Confectionately Yours

Taking the Cake!

Also by Lisa Papademetriou

CANDY APPLE BOOKS

Accidentally Fabulous
Accidentally Famous
Accidentally Fooled
Accidentally Friends
How to Be a Girly Girl in Just Ten Days
Ice Dreams

CONFECTIONATELY YOURS

Save the Cupcake!

OTHER NOVELS

Chasing Normal
Drop
M or F?
Siren's Storm
Sixth-Grade Glommers, Norks, and Me
The Wizard, the Witch, and Two Girls from Jersey

Taking the Cake!

Lisa Papademetriou

SCHOLASTIC INC.

ISBN 978-0-545-22229-7

12 11 10 9 8 7 6 5 4 3 2   12 13 14 15 16 17/0

Printed in the U.S.A.   40

First printing, September 2012

Book design by Yaffa Jaskoll

To Helen Kahn of Cup and Top Cafe in Florence, MA, for her support of local writers and for her fine gluten-free muffins

Taking the Cake!

Slammed

I'm standing at the front of the cafeteria, covered in lasagna. A noodle clings to my shirt for a moment, then drops onto my shoes with a tomato-sauce splat.

Why did I have to get lasagna? I wonder. *Why didn't I get the burger?* But it wouldn't have mattered. I'm also covered in chocolate milk.

"Oops," Artie says. Then she giggles. "Sorry."

"OMG!" Chang lets out a laugh and the two of them walk away.

She didn't do it on purpose, I tell myself as I watch my ex–best friend cross the cafeteria to sit with her new crowd. I really do believe that Artie didn't mean to cover me in lasagna. She'd been chatting with Chang, and neither one of them had been watching where they were going. I'd just gotten my drink. I turned around with my tray, and Artie slammed into me. The tray knocked up against my body, splattering my lunch against my shirt.

I guess I should be grateful that it wasn't soup.

So, no, Artie didn't do it on purpose — but did she really have to laugh?

Artie leans over and says something to Kelley, who is sitting beneath a giant paper jack-o'-lantern. It's Halloween, but nobody's dressed up. Kelley tucks her blond hair behind her ear and casually looks over at me, and then all three girls crack up again. I feel like I've been sliced open. I wonder if the whole cafeteria can see inside my rib cage, where my heart is beating.

I tighten my grip on the orange plastic tray and watch Chang, but she doesn't even glance my way. She has her hand up to the side of her face and she's looking at Artie and laughing.

Artie picks up her lemonade and takes a sip. She looks out into the crowded cafeteria as if she's forgotten me already.

The clink and hum of other students talking and eating surrounds me as everyone else in the cafeteria carries on with their normal lives.

Last year, we learned that scientists found this woolly mammoth frozen solid in a block of ice. They think the Ice

Age may have come on really fast. That's like what's happened to me. Artie used to be my friend. My best friend. And then everything changed.

I turn and walk away. As I head toward the door, I dimly register my other ex–best friend, Marco, sitting with his soccer buddies. There's another mystery: He used to be almost a brother to me. Now he thinks we shouldn't hang out as much.

I don't break my stride as I drop my heavy tray on a nearby table, abandoning my ruined lunch, and push through the double doors. I'm not hungry anymore.

I just want to be alone.

Technically, we aren't supposed to leave the cafeteria during lunch period, but lots of kids do. I walk over to the playing field nearby and sit down in the stands.

Overhead, the sky is a heart-shredding shade of gray. I think about how Artie looked right through me in the cafeteria, and the tears start to flow. I'm crying and crying and my face is wet, and the tears are trickling down my neck and I can't stop crying. I'm trying to be quiet, but I hear someone sit down next to me and I can tell without looking up that it's Marco. I wipe my face, even though he's just staring straight ahead.

"How can she act like that?" I whisper finally.

"I don't know." His eyes flick to mine, then away. He looks like maybe he wants to run, but he stays put beside me.

I shake my head, thinking that I should try to stop crying, or at least stop talking, but I feel my face twisting, and I can't stop the words. "It's like I'm nothing, like I'm worse than something she scraped off her shoe. We were *friends*." I can hardly hear my own words now, because the tears are choking me.

He turns to look at me, and he looks so sad, and so sorry that I feel like another little piece of my heart has been ripped open. "Do you want me to talk to her?" Marco asks.

I laugh a little — a messy laugh, half snort, half snot. "What would you say?"

"I'd say, 'Stop messing with Hayley.'"

"That's not really talking, Marco."

He looks away. "Yeah. I can't think of anything better."

"Me, neither."

He leans toward me then, just a little, until our shoulders are touching. We sit together, just breathing. My arm is warm where it meets his, and I start crying again. Quieter this time. Not as messy. Just tears. I take a deep breath, and my chest feels clean.

The world shifts just a fraction, and even though every-thing's the same as it was five seconds ago, I feel a little better.

"I thought you didn't want to hang out together as much," I say. *Why did you say that?* I wonder. *Things are half-way normal right now — be quiet!*

But Marco just sighs.

"Ohmigosh, what *happened*?"

Meghan Markerson walks up to us with her eyes and mouth round. She's wearing a purple tunic and yellow leggings, and with her newly dyed green bangs and naturally orange hair, she looks kind of like a cartoon character. I don't think it's a costume, though. This is just a normal Meghan outfit.

"Artie accidentally spilled lasagna on me," I say.

"Where is she?" Meghan asks, looking around.

"Inside," Marco explains.

"*What?*" Meghan screeches. "Is she getting you some towels, or something?" She plants a hand on her hip, like, *She'd* better *be getting Hayley some towels.*

Marco looks at me, and I bite my lip.

"She's having lunch," Marco says.

Meghan looks at him for a long moment. Then her eyes narrow, and her nostrils flare.

For some reason, this makes me happy. I've been busy dissolving into tears, but Meghan looks like she wants to go inside and rip Artie's face off. I don't even know Meghan that well, but she's clearly outraged on my behalf. I feel better already.

"Calming breath," Meghan says to herself, inhaling deeply. She closes her eyes, then waves her hands down the length of her body and shakes them out.

"What are you doing?" Marco asks.

"Cleansing my chakras." She hums a little.

Marco and I look at each other. He shrugs. I have no clue, either. Meghan's kind of . . . unique.

Her eyes snap open and she looks at me. "Okay, come on." Meghan holds out a hand.

"Where are we going?" I ask as she drags me up.

"To the gym."

"To work out?" Marco asks. "Lunch is almost over."

"To work out? Are you nuts?" Meghan asks. "No — I've got some spare clothes in my locker."

"You do?" I ask. "Why?"

Meghan looks at me, a little half smile on her face. "Because you never know when you'll get attacked by a lasagna, Hayley."

Marco stands, and his warm, dark eyes meet mine. He punches me on the arm gently, and then turns and heads back into the cafeteria.

"Come on," Meghan says. She's already walking toward the gym, so I follow her.

But I can't help wishing it was Artie leading the way.

Confession:
I Used to Wish that I Was ~~Artie~~

When I was in fourth grade, Apple Laytner decided that she hated my guts. I don't really know why. I told her that I really liked her dad's vegetarian restaurant even though I didn't like vegetables much, and she punched me in the stomach.

For days after that, she was rude to me. She slammed me extra hard on the head with a dodgeball. She tripped me when no one was looking. She had it in for me. I tried to apologize, but she wouldn't stop.

After the dodgeball incident, Artie, Marco, and I walked home together, just like we always did. I told my friends that I didn't know what to do, and I asked them for ideas. Marco said that I should've punched Apple back in the first place, but I'm not really a punching kind of person. Artie just thought it over.

The next day, Artie got all of the girls in our class to ignore Apple completely. After two days, Apple's parents came down to the school and officially complained, but what could our teacher do? You can't make people talk to someone.

It only took one more day for Apple to apologize to me, and after that she left me alone for the rest of the year. The next fall, her parents decided to homeschool her.

Artie was always like a sister to me. She was smart. She cared about me. And I thought she was loyal. I wanted to be like her — just like her.

Now I wonder how much I ever really knew her.

Dirty Work

I don't want to get on the bus that afternoon. Artie's on my bus. Here I am, in flowered leggings and a long black top — Meghan's spare clothes — and I can't take facing my Ex-Best in a borrowed outfit.

It just feels like too much.

So I don't. Instead, I walk home with Meghan. It takes longer, but it's not bad — just a half-hour walk — and it winds past one of the last small farms still in town.

"Oh, thank goodness!" Meghan says as she steps into a pumpkin patch.

I giggle — half because Meghan is such a nut, half because she's making me nervous. "Meghan, you can't just take a pumpkin out of a field without paying for it," I say as she reaches for one.

"Oh, it's no big deal," she says. "It's Halloween — they aren't going to sell these. They're just leaving the pumpkins here to rot because it's good for the soil. But the soil won't miss one."

"That's not the point. The point is that it's not your pumpkin. It's theft."

"Look, I would happily pay for it. I tried to buy one at the farm stand yesterday, but it was closed. The co-op was sold out, and so was State Street Fruit. What am I supposed to do — it's Halloween, and I don't have a pumpkin!" She tries to heft the pumpkin. "Ugh. It's heavy."

"Well, you picked the fattest one."

"My mother always says, 'If you're going to go — go big!'"

"Is she usually referring to criminal activity when she says that?"

"No, she's usually referring to ice cream. But the idea is the same. Help me with this."

"No way."

"Look, just help me get this home, and then I'll go put some money in the frog." There's a frog sculpture in front of First Churches in the middle of downtown Northampton. It has a slot for donations, and any money you put in the frog goes to feed the hungry.

"How much?"

"I don't know." Meghan stands back and surveys the pumpkin. "What would this cost — about eight dollars?"

"Probably."

"Okay, I'll put *ten* dollars in the frog."

Meghan reaches for the pumpkin. It's so heavy that she totters backward, then stumbles onto her rear. She lands in the mud with a splat. The pumpkin rolls onto its side and cracks open.

Meghan bursts into laughter. "Karma! Ugh! I'm covered in pumpkin guts!"

And then — get this — she reaches for another!

"Are you serious?" I demand.

"I've come this far." She grunts as she heaves the pumpkin into the air.

"You are totally insane." She stumbles again, and I rush forward to help her. And just like that, now I'm an accomplice.

"Thanks, Hayley. I don't want to be the only person in town without a jack-o'-lantern."

I sigh. "Fine, but you *have* to feed the frog."

"I will!" Her dimples deepen as she grins. Here is the thing about Meghan Markerson: She can pretty much get anybody to do anything. She even managed to get our school mascot changed. Most of the kids in our class think she's kind of weird, but they usually do whatever she says, anyway.

"Just don't ask for my help robbing any banks," I tell her.

"Please. Look at the lecture I got just for trying to take a pumpkin!"

Between us, it isn't so heavy, but it is a little awkward to carry. Plus, the pumpkin patch is muddy. I trip over half-rotted squash as we squish our way — slowly, carefully — to the edge of the field.

"Let's take a little break," Meghan says. "Put it down on three. One, two —"

And that's when the police car pulls up.

Confession: This Isn't My First Time in a Police Car

Just so you know, they don't have, like, normal backseats. It's a hard fiberglass bench. Maybe uncomfortable seats make people confess? I don't know.

Anyway, yeah, I've been in a police car before. Marco and I got picked up once, when we were in the third grade. We had wandered away from school.

A police officer found us a few blocks away, on Lowell Street.

I remember that the police officer was really nice. She said that we could call her Rosie. She even apologized for making us ride in the back, but she said we weren't allowed to ride in the front.

Rosie let us sit at her desk at the police station until our parents came. Marco's mom got there first. Her face was all red and splotchy, and her voice was hoarse, as if she had been crying her head off. She hugged Marco so hard that I thought she might suffocate him. He looked like he was about to die of embarrassment.

My dad was the one who picked me up. He was all tight lipped and serious, like he didn't know what to say to me. When we got home, he sat me down and told me that what Marco and I had done was stupid. He demanded that I apologize for leaving school.

But I wouldn't.

He sent me to my room, saying that I couldn't have dinner until I came out and apologized. I remember passing my little sister, Chloe, in the hallway on the way up to my room. She was only four years old, and she looked frightened. I wanted to scoop her up and tell her I was okay, nothing bad had happened, but then Dad shouted at me to hurry up, so I just touched her shoulder as I walked past.

During dinner, Mom came upstairs and told me that I could come down and eat the minute I apologized.

I still didn't apologize, though.

The next morning, Dad laid down the law: no breakfast until I apologized.

The smell of eggs and bacon made my stomach rumble, but I still wouldn't do it.

Chloe cried and tried to give me her Cheerios, but Dad wouldn't let her. Mom looked like she was holding back tears. I just sat at the breakfast table, watching Dad. I don't know where I got the guts to do that, but I did.

I didn't apologize until I was about to leave for school. My mom handed me the lunch she had packed. "I'm sorry I scared you," I told her. She touched my hair, then gave me a hug. I squeezed her tight.

I really was sorry.

But I still wouldn't apologize to Dad.

Marco and I weren't *stupid*, and I wasn't about to agree with Dad and say that we were. I wouldn't.

And I never did.

Heat

The warm café is a relief from the chill autumn air as Officer Martinez and I step inside. When the bell jingles, Gran looks up, smiling. "Well, Hayley, I see you've made a friend," she says warmly, as if it's perfectly normal that I would hang out with a uniformed police officer.

Mom — who was sitting at a table near the back, working on her laptop — stands up. For a moment, she is still as a stone, her mouth open and eyes wide. Then she hurries over to us. "Are you hurt?" she asks me, and before I can answer, she wraps me in a hug.

"I'm fine." My words are muffled by the fabric of her shirt.

She pulls back and smoothes my hair away from my face, then looks up at the officer. "What — ?"

"The farmers have declined to press charges," he says.

If Mom were a cartoon, her eyes would be sproinging out of her head.

"Meghan wanted a pumpkin, and there wasn't any place to buy one, so I helped her. . . ." Oh, this sounds lame, even to me. "Sorry."

"Pumpkin theft," Gran says. "And on Halloween. Who's heard of such madness?" My grandmother is from England. Here is the truth: Sarcasm sounds extra hilarious when it comes from an old British lady, so — naturally — I giggle.

Mom frowns, and I clamp my lips together.

Officer Martinez's thick black mustache twitches, but Mom doesn't smile. "Thank you for bringing her home safely," she says, trying to smooth down her wild, dark curls.

"It was my pleasure," Officer Martinez tells her.

There's an awkward moment when I wonder just how grounded I'll be for my role as Accessory to Pumpkin Theft. Probably extremely grounded, even though the farmers — a young hippie couple — were pretty amused by our crime.

"Could we . . . could we offer you a scone?" Mom asks the police officer. "A cup of coffee?"

"On the house, of course," Gran adds, giving him a twinkly-eyed smile.

"Those scones do smell delicious," he says. "But I'm happy to pay for one."

"Oh, no — really, let us thank you." Mom hurries behind the counter.

Officer Martinez is already reaching for his wallet. "I appreciate it, but I can't accept."

"Oh." Mom's eyebrows go up in surprise. "Oh — because it might seem like a bribe?"

"I never take anything for free from a civilian," the officer tells her. "Not even a stick of gum."

Officer Martinez smiles as he hands Mom the money for the scone. "Don't be too hard on her," he tells Mom. "Her friend confessed that it was her idea — and I think they're both sorry."

"Hayley needs to learn to use better judgment," Mom says sternly. "But thank you, Officer Martinez."

"Ramon," he says.

Mom looks a little surprised. "Margaret."

"Pleased to meet you." Ramon pulls the scone out of the wax paper bag and takes a bite as he walks to the door. "Delicious," he says as he backs through the exit. Then he smiles again and steps out onto the street. Mom watches him as he walks past the window.

"Mom?"

She looks at me as if she's trying to remember who I am. I guess my run-in with the law has left her dazed. I don't blame her. I'm feeling pretty dazed, too.

At that moment, my sister, Chloe, and her friend Rupert slam through the front door. Rupert is dressed as an astronaut.

"What are you supposed to be?" I ask my little sister. "A hamburger?"

Rupert snorts.

"I'm the planet *Saturn*," Chloe corrects, as if it is the most obvious thing in the world. "When are we leaving to go trick-or-treating?"

"Hayley isn't going," Mom announces. "She's grounded."

"What?" Chloe gives Mom the Big Baby-Animal Eyes. "That isn't fair!"

"Tell it to Hayley," Mom says.

So Chloe gives *me* the Big Baby-Animal Eyes.

"I'm so sorry," I tell my sister.

"Surely Chloe and Rupert are old enough to go by themselves," Gran offers.

Mom looks dubious.

"My sisters can take us," Rupert announces in his quiet voice.

Chloe looks at him. "But what about Hayley? Halloween is only once a year," she says. "She's going to miss it!"

Then she turns to me, and she looks so sad and so sorry for me that I wrap her in a hug, which isn't easy in that Saturn outfit. "It's okay, Chlo," I say.

She lets go and stands back. "What are you wearing?" she asks. "Is that a costume?"

I realize suddenly that I've still got on Meghan's spare leggings and shirt. "Oh, that's a whole other story."

"Your sister will survive, Chloe," Mom says.

"She'll watch the parade here, with me," Gran puts in.

"She's grounded, Mother," Mom explains.

"Well, surely that doesn't mean she won't be allowed to help her grandmother?" Gran smiles, all innocence.

Mom sighs. "I need to ground your grandma," she says to me, but I can tell that she's joking, and that everything is all right. "No computer and no TV for the rest of the week. And no trick-or-treating tonight."

"Phone?" I ask.

"Only if it's me or your dad."

"Or your beloved grandmama," Gran adds.

I sigh. "What about homework — can I use the computer?" I ask.

"Yes, but I'll be watching." She storms back to her table to resume her work.

My sister gives me a last squeeze, and she and Rupert head out the door. To find his sisters, I guess.

When things get this bad, there's only one thing to do, so I head behind the counter to bake cupcakes.

Modern Carrot-Cake Cupcakes

(makes approximately 12 cupcakes)

Is there anything more comforting than carrot cake? Bonus: counts as a vegetable!

INGREDIENTS:

- 1 cup finely grated carrots
- 1/3 cup yogurt (plain or vanilla)
- 1 teaspoon vanilla extract
- 1/3 cup granulated sugar
- 1/3 cup brown sugar
- 1/3 cup canola oil
- 3/4 cup gluten-free all-purpose flour, such as Bob's Red Mill
- 1/4 teaspoon baking powder
- 1 teaspoon baking soda
- 1/4 teaspoon salt
- 1/4 teaspoon ground cinnamon
- 1/4 teaspoon ground ginger
- 1/2 teaspoon ground cardamom
- 1/4 cup chopped toasted pistachio nuts
- 1/4 cup golden raisins, soaked in orange juice for 10 minutes

INSTRUCTIONS:

1. Preheat the oven to 350°F. Line a muffin pan with cupcake liners.

2. In a large bowl, using a whisk or handheld mixer, mix together the grated carrots, yogurt, vanilla extract, granulated sugar, brown sugar, and oil.

3. In a separate bowl, sift together the gluten-free flour, baking powder, baking soda, salt, cinnamon, ginger, and cardamom.

4. Add the dry ingredients to the wet ones a little bit at a time, stopping to scrape the sides of the bowl a few times, and mix until no lumps remain. Add the chopped pistachio nuts and golden raisins, and combine completely.

5. Fill cupcake liners two-thirds of the way and bake for 18–22 minutes. Transfer to a cooling rack, and let cool completely before frosting.

Spiced Cream-Cheese Frosting

INGREDIENTS:

1/4 cup cream cheese, softened to room temperature

1/4 cup margarine or butter, softened to room temperature

2 cups confectioners' sugar

1 teaspoon vanilla extract

1/4 teaspoon ground cardamom

1/4 teaspoon ground ginger

INSTRUCTIONS:

1. In a bowl, using a handheld mixer, cream together the cream cheese and margarine or butter completely. Slowly add the confectioners' sugar in 1/2-cup batches, mixing completely before adding more.

2. Add the vanilla extract, cardamom, and ginger, and beat on high speed until the frosting becomes light and fluffy, about 3–7 minutes.

EmandEm12: I'm grounded.

Cupcakegirlie: Me too. Got to keep this short — Mom's watching!

EmandEm12: Same. I'm sorry!

Cupcakegirlie: It's okay.

EmandEm12: Why on earth did you let me steal that pumpkin?

Cupcakegirlie: You're kidding?????

EmandEm12: Yes! Don't kill me! Not all of my ideas are winners.

Cupcakegirlie: Snort.

EmandEm12: Are you going to get over this?

Cupcakegirlie: Not right away.

EmandEm12: How long? Days? Weeks?

Cupcakegirlie: I'll probably be fine tomorrow. You're such a nutburger.
EmandEm12: Good!
Cupcakegirlie: Now stop IMing!! G2G!
EmandEm12: C U!

Costumes

"I think my favorite so far is the jellyfish," Gran announces, then sips her tea.

"Oh, yes, very creative," Mr. Malik agrees as he takes a bite of carrot cupcake. "But I admire the suffragette." He nods approvingly at a ten-year-old girl in a long skirt and high-necked blouse carrying a VOTES FOR WOMEN! sign.

We're watching the Halloween parade flow down the street past our shop window. There are endless costumes — some clearly store-bought, others sewn by hand or crafted with a few creative household materials. One girl is dressed as a robot, with a sign that lights up when you put candy in her bucket. A group of boys are dressed as Lord of the Rings characters: a couple of Orcs, Legolas, and Frodo. From babies to grannies — the whole town turns out for the Halloween parade.

"I like the groups," I say as three superheroines strut past. They're obviously high schoolers, and clearly at least one of them has some mad sewing skills. Wonder Woman, Batgirl, and Supergirl all have excellent costumes. Wonder Woman even has a golden lasso. And with them are . . . an astronaut and the planet Saturn?

"Oh — they must be Rupert's sisters," Gran says, beaming. She waves, and Rupert waves back. Chloe smiles and makes a goofy face at us through the glass.

"I didn't realize his sisters were —" I stop myself.

"Caucasian?" Mr. Malik finishes for me.

"Well, yeah," I admit. Rupert's skin is dark brown, and these girls are pale with golden hair. "And they're so much older."

"You can never predict a family," Gran points out.

Just then, the bell over the door jingles. Time seems to freeze as Artie walks in.

What's she doing here? I think. I mean, she knows this is Gran's tea shop. For a crazy moment, I think that maybe she's come to apologize for the lasagna incident, but a moment later, Devon McAllister appears behind her. Cold numbness crawls up my body, starting at my feet. His blue eyes lock with mine for a moment, and I forget how to breathe.

"Hi!" His smile shoots through me like a mild electric current, and I manage to thaw enough to wave at him.

"Hello, Hayley." Artie flashes me a huge smile as she steps up to the counter. "I told Devon he just had to try one of your cupcakes."

I blink a few times, trying to make sense of her words, but I'm distracted by the small white spot at the bottom of Devon's right front tooth. It's so cute, and I can't believe I've never noticed it before. I suddenly realize that Artie has cocked her head and is waiting for me to say something. "You guys aren't going trick-or-treating?" I ask.

"I know, bummer, right?" Devon says just as Artie says, "Is that a joke?" Her smug little smile says it all: *We're a little too mature for that, aren't we?* I feel like an idiot.

"I couldn't get a costume together," Devon admits. "Besides, I've got to get home and finish my homework." He flashes me a smile that makes me think that maybe I'm not an idiot, after all.

It's very odd to think that I have more in common with Devon than with my Ex-Best.

Artie frowns a little, but Devon doesn't see it, because he's making his way over to the glass display case. My head is spinning. *What is happening right now?* I wonder. I get the feeling that Artie and Devon's appearance at the café means something, but I have no idea what.

"Wow — ginger and chocolate. I'll try one of those." Devon's brilliant blue eyes land on mine, and I feel myself turning into a puddle. "Sounds awesome."

"Muh," I say. Somebody get a mop, because Devon is making my brain leak out of my ears.

Artie bats her eyes at him. "That does sound good," she says. "But I think I'll go for the vanilla bean." I grab a sheet of wax paper and reach for the cupcakes as my grandmother joins us. *Is this some sort of Artie Apology?* I wonder.

"Hello, Artemis," Gran says with her usual smile. "We haven't seen you for a while."

"I've been busy — Devon and I are in the school musical," Artie says. Her hand reaches for his fingers, and she flashes me a smug little smile.

My skin goes cold as everything suddenly clicks into place — *Artie has come here to make me feel bad.* It's as if the thought has dropped out of a tree and landed with a thunk against my skull. *She knows I have a crush on Devon — she wants to make me jealous.*

I feel my eyes burning.

This is worse than the lasagna.

Now she's just being mean.

My guts churn and my face burns as I hand over the cupcakes. "Here you go." I ring them up, and they take the table right by the window. Blocking my view of the parade, just so you know.

I wipe down the counter, trying hard not to stare at my ex–best friend as she gazes adoringly at Devon. She looks over at me and blinks her eyes slowly, like a cat.

"What a handsome young man," Gran murmurs.

My face turns to fire, and I use the rag to scrub extra hard at a sticky stain.

"Oh, yes," Mr. Malik agrees. "All youth is loveliness." He gives me a warm smile that lights up his dark eyes. He owns the flower shop next door and is Gran's good friend. He is from Pakistan, and he and Gran get along because they're both very British. But he's also like an extra grandfather to me. Of course he thinks that all youth is loveliness. Right. Only some youth is more loveliness than others. Artie has hazel eyes and gleaming auburn hair. She looks like she should have her own TV show, or skin-care line, or something.

I, on the other hand, usually have cupcake batter in my hair.

Devon watches the parade of costumes, laughing at some of the clever ones and pointing out anything interesting to Artie. But she doesn't seem to want to look at anything but Devon.

As the parade slows to a trickle, the Tea Room starts to fill up with customers. Most are moms wanting pre-trick-or-treating coffee. Coffee is candy for grown-ups, I guess. For a while, Gran and I are so busy that I forget Artie and Devon are even there. Sort of. The way you forget a mosquito that's buzzing in your ear.

Things start to slow down, and I go around, wiping tables and clearing away trash.

"Hey, Hayley!" Devon waves at me. I glance over at Artie, who is scowling.

"Hayley, this is the best cupcake I've ever had!" Devon gushes as I walk up to their table. "What did you put in it?"

Seriously, at that moment I can't think of a single thing that went into any of my cupcakes. His handsomeness is that intense: It actually causes my brain to short-circuit. "Oh, uh — secret ingredients."

Devon laughs like I've just made the best joke ever. I feel my stomach flip as his blue eyes crinkle with laughter. "Man, they're awesome! Right, Artemis?"

"Mmm." Artie gives a tight-lipped little nod. She smiles at me, but it looks strained.

I'm getting the feeling that their trip to the Tea Room isn't going the way she'd planned.

"So — you make up the recipes yourself?" Devon asks.

"Yeah. Most of them are inspired by other recipes," I admit. "But I like to experiment, mix up flavors."

"It must be cool to have a talent like that," Devon says.

"*You're* amazingly talented," Artie gushes.

This is actually true. Devon is a terrific actor — he's in all the school plays.

Devon waves his hand. "Oh, I meant a talent for something *useful*. I mean, you can't eat a play — right, Hayley?" And he gives me a smile that makes me feel like I'm standing in a beam of sunlight.

Artie frowns. "Isn't it time for us to get going? Weren't we planning to run lines tonight?"

"Oh, sure," Devon says. He reaches for his plate, but Artie tells him to leave it.

"Hayley will clean it up — right, Hayley?" Her lip curls.

"Right," I say, resisting the urge to throttle her. *Why does she have to act like that?* I wonder as Artie flounces out the door. It's almost like *she's* jealous, or something.

But that's dumb. I mean, Artie and I aren't really friends

anymore . . . but that doesn't mean I'd ever try to steal Devon.

Even if he is gorgeous. And talented. And even if he does like my cupcakes.

And even if Artie has turned into a horrible person who deserves to get revenged.

I'm just not that kind of person.

Math Problems

Marco's sitting in the second row of the school bus when I get on. Artie is there, too, in the back row. Chang Xiao is in my Ex-Seat.

I kind of think Artie is a jerk, but sometimes I wish we were still friends. Does that sound weird? I guess I wish I could go back in time to the way things used to be.

I scan the seats, hoping for one that's completely empty. No use. I'm the last person to get on the bus — every seat has at least one person in it. So I plop down in the spot beside Marco, who doesn't look up from his math book. His notebook is open, and I can see he's been struggling with the homework.

"Why would I ever have to write something in scientific notation?" Marco demands.

I consider this a moment. "Um, because you're a scientist?"

He looks at me evenly, with those calm black eyes of his. "Let's say that I'm a professional soccer player — now why would I need scientific notation?"

"To graduate from middle school?"

He sighs. "Then I may not graduate from middle school."

"It's not that hard," I tell him. "You're overthinking it. Look." I pull out my notebook and turn to the homework. "See, you just need to count the decimal places."

I work with him for a while, until the bus pulls up in front of the school. Unfortunately, Mr. Carter assigned forty problems.

Marco looks panicked. "Still thirty more."

"Why didn't you work on it at home?" I ask.

"I *did*," Marco insists. "But it took me forever to finish the reading for English, and then there were those social studies questions. . . ." He runs an impatient hand through his dark, floppy hair. "Listen, Hayley, can I borrow this homework? Just for homeroom — then I'll give it back."

It's not copying, I tell myself. It's *helping* him. Besides, if he doesn't finish, Mr. Carter will give him a zero. Homework is sacred to Mr. Carter. His motto is "Much and Often," and he counts your homework grade as fifty percent of your final grade.

And besides, Marco is my friend. Am I really going to tell him no?

"Sure, Marco." I pass him my notebook, still open to the homework. "No problem."

Confession:
Mr. Carter Is a Dirtbag

I know I shouldn't say that about my teacher. I should have respect for him. And I try. I really do.

But he's *mean.*

He doesn't look mean. On the first day of class, I thought I was lucky. Mr. Carter is young — for a teacher — and has blue eyes and thin blond hair that's starting to pull back from his forehead like a wave returning to the ocean. He dresses well, always in khaki pants and a button-down shirt that looks like it was ironed by someone who knows what they're doing. That first day, he looked like the ideal teacher — organized, young, and reasonably smart. But that wasn't the whole story.

Mr. Carter isn't the kind of teacher who's mean to everyone. I have one of those, too — Miss Timmons, who's about twice as old as Yoda and has the same wardrobe. But I don't think *she's* a dirtbag. She's mean, but she's fair about it. She's mean to *everyone equally*. Mr. Carter, on the other hand, plays favorites: He's only mean to the kids who aren't good at math. Here's the thing — I'm good at math, so Mr. Carter leaves me alone. But I still think he's a dirtbag.

Yesterday, he was teaching us the basics of scientific notation. Mr. Carter read the concept out of the book, and then wrote a problem on the board. He asked if anyone wanted to come up and show us how to work it. I put up my hand. So did five other people. But who did he call on?

Marco.

Marco looked up, his lips pressed together grimly. It wasn't the first time Mr. Carter had called on him when Marco was clearly lost. In fact, this is one of our teacher's favorite tricks. So, as usual, Marco trooped up to the whiteboard, book in hand. He picked up a marker and stared at the problem for a moment, hesitating. I could hear the blood rushing in my ears.

"What's the matter, Marco?" Mr. Carter asked. "You can't count?" His face was this ugly sneer, lip curled. "Go sit down. Tanisha, can you help us?"

Tanisha Osborne nearly jumped out of her seat. Marco handed her the marker, and she did her usual Tanisha Technique of narrating how she arrived at the answer while she solved the problem. "Okay, so, if we're looking for the scientific notation of 3,750, first we take the first digit —" And blah, blah, blah. She wasn't trying to be annoying, but she *was* succeeding.

Marco just looked at the floor all the way back to his desk. Scientific notation isn't even the hardest thing we've done all year. But I don't think Marco is trying anymore. I wouldn't, if Mr. Carter had embarrassed me as often as he's humiliated Marco.

So part of me is *glad* that I gave Marco my homework. Maybe he'll see that this stuff isn't so hard. Maybe it'll help him understand.

Besides — like I said — Mr. Carter is a total dirtbag. If he were a better teacher, this wouldn't be my problem.

Light Speed

"Einstein said it," Meghan is saying as I plop my lunch tray beside hers and take a seat. "I believe it. End of story." She crunches into a stick of celery, as if that's the last word on the subject.

I recognize the boy across the table from her: Ben Habib. He's super cute, in a nerdy way. He's got huge black eyes and short black hair cropped close to his head and rectangular glasses. But he's so shy, I don't think I've ever exchanged more than two words with him.

"But the equations show that it's possible that neutrons move more quickly than light," Ben says. "Aren't you even interested? Hi, Hayley," he adds as an aside.

"Hi."

"I'm not buying it," Meghan insists, ignoring me while

simultaneously making space for me beside her. "They'll find a mistake in the calculations. Mark my words." She stabs the air with her celery.

Ben laughs softly. "Consider them marked." He stands up, flashes me a silvery braces smile, and heads over to a table full of his friends.

Meghan lays her head on her palm and munches her celery dreamily. "He's so amazing," she says with a sigh. She turns to me and demands, "How many people in this school like to talk about Einstein?"

"Two," I tell her. "You guys were made for each other."

I actually don't mean anything romantic by this comment, but Meghan blushes. Her pink skin looks pretty with the green bangs and wisps framing her face. Meghan is no great beauty. She has a round, chubby-cheeked face and a wide nose. But she's always wearing something funky, and she's almost irresistibly cute. "I'm going to tell him how I feel," she announces.

I nearly choke on the pizza I'm eating. Meghan told me a few weeks ago that she was crushed out on Ben. I guess I hadn't really realized how serious she was. I chew for a moment, then ask, "Is that a good idea?"

"No," Meghan admits. "It's a horrible idea."

Meghan takes a sip of milk, then stares off into space, eyes narrowed, for a few moments. "I'm going to do it, anyway."

"Meg —"

"I'll send him a secret-admirer letter."

"Still a bad idea," I inform her.

"Yes, but not *as* bad." How can she cheerfully agree with me while simultaneously pulling a piece of paper out of her messenger bag? How? She scribbles *Dear Ben* at the top, then draws a heart.

"You're a lunatic!"

"Relax, Hayley — this isn't pumpkin theft! No laws are broken, nobody gets hurt." Her dimples show as she scribbles away.

I take another bite of pizza to stop myself from saying, "Except maybe you."

What should I do? I wonder. Grab the paper and toss it in the trash? "At least wait until tomorrow before you give that to him," I say.

"I'll pop it in his locker at the end of the day." She starts folding the note into an elaborate shape. For a few moments, I can't tell what it is. Finally, it takes form — a heart with wings.

I decide not to say anything else. Arguing with Meghan is like arguing with a truck that's about to run you over: You may have a good point, but that's not going to stop it.

Maybe she'll forget about it by the end of the day, I hope. *Maybe she'll change her mind.*

"So what about you, Hayley?" Meghan asks. "What about Devon?"

"Shhh!"

Meghan laughs. "Nobody's listening!" she insists as I look over my shoulder.

She's right. Nobody is paying the slightest bit of attention to us. Besides, the cafeteria is so noisy, we might as well be in a soundproof booth.

"I don't know," I admit finally. "He came to the café yesterday."

"Oooh!" She lifts her eyebrows.

"With Artie."

"Eeew."

"Yeah, exactly." I take another bite of pizza.

"Wow — she's so jealous of you," Meghan says, which makes me choke on my pizza again.

"Jealous? Are you living in a parallel universe right now? She thinks I'm scum."

Meghan shrugs. "Okay."

"Why would she be jealous of me?"

"Because you're funny and smart and make awesome cupcakes?" Meghan suggests. "And because people like you, and they think Artie's an idiot?"

"Lots of people like Artie."

"Okay," Meghan says again, with that same little shrug.

I don't know whether I want to hug her or toss my pizza at her. She's nuts. There is no way Artie's jealous of me.

Still, it's sweet of her to think so.

From the Phone Files: Part 1

"Hello?"

"Hayley, it's Dad."

"I know, Dad. Remember caller ID? How are you?"

"I'm great. What's new?"

"Not much. So — hey, can we go hiking on Saturday? All the leaves are about to finish changing colors. It might be our last chance."

"Sure, sure — but I wanted to talk about Thanksgiving."

"What about it?"

"Well, Annie's parents have invited us to join them at their country club for dinner. . . . Hello? Are you there?"

"I'm just — for Thanksgiving dinner?"

"Yes."

"What about Mom?"

"We agreed we would share holidays."

"Okay . . . but . . . Thanksgiving in a restaurant? Doesn't that seem —"

"Lots of people have Thanksgiving in a restaurant. That way you don't have to have turkey. You can have whatever you like."

"I like turkey."

"You can have turkey."

"With Annie?"

"Look, Hayley, it was a very nice gesture for her parents to invite us out to their country club. I expect you to say so when you meet them."

"So — it sounds like we're going."

"We are."

"Okay. Um, where is it?"

"Connecticut."

"So they're rich."

"Not everyone in Connecticut is rich."

"So they're not rich?"

"No — listen, Hayley, that's not the point."

"Do you want to talk to Chloe?"

"I'd like to talk to you some more."

"I don't really have any news."

"Okay, Hayley. Fine. You can put Chloe on. Love you."

"Bye."

Rain Forest Cupcakes

(makes approximately 12 cupcakes)

Sometimes what you really need is a tropical vacation. But when you can't have one, a tropical cupcake can work, too.

INGREDIENTS:

    1 medium very ripe banana, mashed well
    2/3 cup coconut milk
    1 teaspoon coconut extract
    1/2 teaspoon vanilla extract
    1/2 cup granulated sugar
    1/4 cup brown sugar
    1/3 cup canola oil
    1-1/4 cups flour
    1 teaspoon baking powder
    1/4 teaspoon baking soda
    1/2 teaspoon salt
    1/2 cup chopped toasted macadamia nuts
    1/2 cup semisweet chocolate chips

INSTRUCTIONS:

1. Preheat the oven to 350°F. Line a muffin pan with cupcake liners.
2. In a small bowl, whisk together the banana, coconut milk, coconut extract, vanilla extract, granulated sugar, brown sugar, and oil.
3. In a larger bowl, sift together the flour, baking powder, baking soda, and salt, and mix.
4. Add the dry ingredients to the wet ones a little bit at a time, and combine with a whisk or handheld mixer, stopping to scrape the sides of the bowl a few times, until no lumps remain. Add the chopped macadamia nuts and chocolate chips, and combine completely.
5. Fill cupcake liners two-thirds of the way and bake for 18–22 minutes. Transfer to a cooling rack, and let cool completely before frosting.

Peanut Butter–Butterscotch Frosting

INGREDIENTS:

    1/2 cup butterscotch chips

    1/2 cup margarine or butter

    1/3 cup creamy peanut butter

    1 teaspoon vanilla extract

    2 cups confectioners' sugar

INSTRUCTIONS:

1. Melt the butterscotch chips in a small bowl in the microwave, then set aside to cool to room temperature.
2. In another bowl, using a handheld mixer, cream together the margarine or butter with the peanut butter until completely combined. Add the vanilla extract, and then slowly add the confectioners' sugar in 1/2-cup batches, mixing completely before adding more.
3. Add the melted butterscotch and beat on high speed until the frosting becomes light and fluffy, about 3–7 minutes.

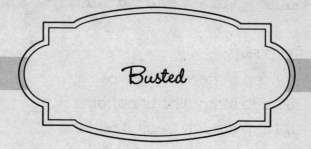

Busted

The bell over the door jingles, and I look up from frosting my French-toast cupcakes. A dark-haired man with a mustache is standing at the counter. He's wearing a button-down shirt and a brown corduroy jacket with jeans, and he looks familiar. . . .

"Well, hullo!" Gran says cheerfully. "Came back for another scone, I see."

I nearly drop my cupcake when I realize that it's Officer Ramirez.

He smiles. "And a cup of coffee, please."

"I'm glad you policemen don't all fancy doughnuts." Gran nods in approval.

"I love doughnuts," Chloe pipes up from her perch at the end of the counter. "But they aren't as good as Gran's scones."

"Or Hayley's cupcakes," Rupert adds.

I gape at him. Rupert has started talking more, but it always surprises me when he does.

"You should make doughnut cupcakes," Chloe suggests.

"What's that?" I ask. "A cupcake with a hole in the middle?"

"No clue. That's your job. Figure it out — and when you make them, you can tell everyone it was my idea."

Officer Ramirez laughs just as my mother comes out from the back room, frowning at the phone. She stops in her tracks when she sees him, then smiles. It's a tight smile, though, like it's covering something.

I nibble my fingernail, then get annoyed with myself, because now I have to wash my hands before I can go back to frosting the cupcakes.

"Is everything all right, Margaret?" Gran asks as she passes Officer Ramirez his scone.

"It's just —" Mom waves her hand, then huffs out a sigh. "I just got off the phone with William. He wants to take the girls on Thanksgiving."

Gran looks indignant. "Well, he can't!"

Mom smiles a little sadly. "It was part of the terms of the divorce, Mother."

"We aren't going to have Thanksgiving with you?" Chloe looks like she's about to cry.

Mom touches her arm. "You will, sweetie. You'll have dinner with us here, at noon. Then you and Hayley can join him afterward."

I feel my heart sink. I'm not sure I want to have two Thanksgivings. I was really just hoping that the one with my dad's new girlfriend's family would get canceled. I mean, does that sound Thanksgiving-ish to you?

"It's good you agreed to share the holiday," Officer Ramirez puts in. Not that anyone has asked him. "I don't get to see my son at all on Thanksgiving."

Chloe is aghast. "You spend Thanksgiving *alone*?"

"I usually volunteer at the soup kitchen," Officer Ramirez explains. "It puts things in perspective." He looks at his mug, then takes a long sip of his coffee.

We're all quiet for a moment.

"I wish I could spend Thanksgiving alone," Rupert says suddenly. "Instead, all of my Polish relatives come over and pinch my cheeks and holler and laugh and sing. It's *noisy*."

"You don't like noise?" Gran asks.

Rupert shakes his head. "I like to *read*."

"Well, at least they're your family," I say to him. "And you have just one Thanksgiving."

Chloe stares down at the floor.

"Hayley —" Mom starts, but I tug off my apron and place it on the counter.

"I'm going out for some air." The door jingles as I push my way out onto the street.

Two Thanksgivings.

I like turkey — but not *that* much.

Confession: The Top Five Things I Love about Thanksgiving

5. Watching the Thanksgiving Day Parade on TV. Be sure to check out the people who dance in the street around the floats. They're always dressed as presents or candy canes, or something else equally ridiculous. You can tell they hate it — it's awesome!

4. Gran's cinnamon buns, which we always have for breakfast that day.

3. Post-turkey walk. We used to walk around our neighborhood after dinner. Some people have Christmas lights up already, and it's lovely.

2. Playing the Thankful Game. We go around in a circle, naming things we're thankful for. Each person has to remember what everyone before has said, then add something new. We usually go around two or three times, and it's nice to remember how much we have to be happy about.

1. Stuffing. Mom just uses the kind that comes in a box, but it's sooooo gooooood.

So — those are the things I'm thankful for. But . . . are we even doing those things this year? We'll be off at some random country club while we're supposed to be on our walk. And we'll probably have to eat our first turkey while the parade is still happening. Will Gran make the cinnamon buns? Will we have time to play our game?

I think I can count on the stuffing, at least.

Even so, this is starting to sound like a holiday I barely recognize — one where the fun things have been sucked away, and only the name remains.

Am I supposed to find a way to be thankful for this?

Because I'm trying.

But it's not working.

Cornbread Cupcakes
(makes approximately 12 cupcakes)

Ah, cornbread. Just like the Pilgrims would've had . . . you know, if they'd had cupcakes.

INGREDIENTS:
- 2 tablespoons brown sugar
- 1/4 cup honey
- 1/2 teaspoon Chinese five-spice powder
- 1 cup chopped toasted pecans
- 1 cup milk
- 1 teaspoon apple cider vinegar
- 1-1/2 teaspoons vanilla extract
- 1/2 cup granulated sugar
- 1/3 cup canola oil
- 2 tablespoons maple syrup
- 3/4 cup gluten-free all-purpose flour, such as Bob's Red Mill
- 1/2 cup cornmeal
- 3/4 teaspoon baking powder
- 1/2 teaspoon baking soda
- 1/2 teaspoon salt

INSTRUCTIONS:

1. Preheat the oven to 350°F. Line a muffin pan with cupcake liners.
2. In a small skillet over low heat, melt together the brown sugar, honey, Chinese five-spice powder, and pecans until the sugar is fully dissolved, then remove from heat and set aside the syrupy pecans to cool.
3. Mix the milk and vinegar in a bowl and let sit a few minutes to curdle. Once curdled, add the vanilla extract, granulated sugar, oil, and maple syrup.
4. In another bowl, sift together the flour, cornmeal, baking powder, baking soda, and salt, and mix.
5. Add the dry ingredients to the wet ones a little bit at a time, and combine with a whisk or handheld mixer until smooth, stopping to scrape the sides of the bowl a few times. Add the syrupy pecans and stir a few times to marbleize the batter.
6. Fill the cupcake liners two-thirds of the way and bake for 20–22 minutes. Transfer the cupcakes to a cooling rack, and let cool completely before frosting.

Mascarpone Frosting

INGREDIENTS:

- 8 ounces mascarpone cheese
- 1/2 cup margarine or butter, softened to room temperature
- 2-1/2 cups confectioners' sugar
- 1 teaspoon vanilla extract

INSTRUCTIONS:

1. In a bowl, using a handheld mixer, cream together the mascarpone cheese and margarine or butter completely. Slowly add the confectioners' sugar in 1/2-cup batches, mixing completely before adding more.

2. Add the vanilla extract and beat on high speed until the frosting becomes light and fluffy, about 3–7 minutes.

Like Crazy

$\mathcal{M}$eghan and I are sitting on the steps of city hall, watching people go by and drinking hot apple cider while we munch on the gluten-free cupcakes I've made for us both. Meghan has celiac disease, so she can't have wheat and certain other grains. I have to be really careful when I bake for her — even just a trace of flour could make her super sick. (We made these at her house.) But she's so grateful whenever I make her a cupcake that I'm happy to do it.

We're playing "Love It Like Crazy!" which is a game I made up where you point out clothes or accessories or whatever that are either really cool or really hideous. It's one of those perfect fall days — cool, but not cold. Crisp, with a blue sky and scudding white clouds.

"Love those boots like crazy!" Meghan says to me, nodding at a woman in a pair of neon-green cowboy boots. They're way cool.

"Love that hat like crazy," I add, because the same woman is wearing a fabulous cheetah-print hat.

"Yeah, she's got style." Meghan grins. "Love this cupcake like crazy," she says as she polishes it off.

"Thanks." I smile and take another bite. Honestly, they really did turn out well.

"Love that bandanna like crazy," Meghan notes. A cute Australian shepherd prances by, rainbow scarf around his neck. Adorable.

A bald guy is holding the dog's leash. I whisper, "Love those face piercings like crazy."

"Ooh, yeah, and the snake tattoo. Like crazy!"

Ugh. She's right. It's the worst tattoo ever, like maybe the guy let his five-year-old draw it up the back of his neck. We break into giggles . . . but not too loudly, because the guy looks like he could easily rip our arms off.

Meghan takes a sip of hot cider. She spots something, and her eyes narrow.

I follow her gaze to see Artie and Devon crossing the street toward us. Artie is holding a bag from Faces in one hand. The other is resting on Devon's arm. She's gazing at him, but Devon is waving at us. Me, specifically.

"Hayley!" Devon calls. He quickens his pace, and Artie's hand falls from his arm. "I'm so glad we ran into you! Hi, Meghan."

"Hey, Devon. Hey, Artie," Meghan says.

"Artemis," she corrects. Artie flashes us a thin smile, as if she can barely endure our presence. It's a real ego boost to get a look like that from someone who used to be your best friend, let me tell you. Love it like crazy!

Meghan takes another sip of her cider, then leans back on her elbows, sort of draped casually across the steps. She doesn't reply to Artie's name change.

"Have you had one of Hayley's cupcakes?" Devon asks Meghan. "They're amazing! Right, Artemis?"

I feel myself flush with happiness, but Artie just nods. "Mmm."

"Hayley makes me gluten-free cupcakes," Meghan replies. "I just had one that was literally the best thing I've eaten in three years."

"So, I had this brilliant idea, Hayley," Devon says. "How about you come up with some original, crazy cupcakes to sell as a fund-raiser for the musical?"

"For the musical?" Artie's eyebrows fly up. I can read her mind: *You mean* my *musical?*

"Why not?" Devon says. "I mean, you guys are good friends, right?"

We look at each other for a moment. "Oh, *right*," Artie replies.

I give a tight little smile and a shrug that could mean anything.

Artie hesitates. "Still, I'm not sure Hayley has the time. . . ."

I'm not wild about the idea, either. The fact is, Artie and I *aren't* friends anymore, and she clearly doesn't want me busting in on her Devon Time. "We're not allowed to have bake sales at school anymore," I point out.

"Right!" Artie says.

"Yeah, but you could sell them during the play, at intermission," Devon suggests. "We always sell treats then. It isn't during official school hours. Why don't you come to rehearsal tomorrow and we can suggest the cupcake idea to Ms. Lang. Then you can stay and watch. Maybe it'll help you come up with a few ideas —"

The whole time Devon is saying this, Artie is scowling at me like it's my fault that the World's Cutest Guy likes my cupcakes. "Devon, the drama club can just sell candy," she snaps. "Hayley doesn't have to come to our rehearsals and go crazy baking —"

"It sounds like fun." I don't know what makes me say this. Maybe an evil part of me just wants to see Artie squirm, the way she made me squirm the other day.

"What?" Artie's head snaps toward me. "Aren't you too busy, Hayley?" she asks through clenched teeth.

"I'm never too busy to help a friend!" I say in my sweetest voice.

"Isn't she the greatest, Devon?" Meghan asks.

"Definitely!" Devon says.

"Oh, yes, definitely," Artie echoes faintly.

"So we'll see you tomorrow?" Devon asks. "Four P.M. — the rehearsal's in the auditorium."

"I'll be there," I promise.

"Awesome!" Devon says, and he and Artie walk off.

Meghan grins and throws her arm across my shoulders. "Love that Hayley like crazy!" she shouts after them, and we both crack up. "Well, it looks like young Mr. McAllister is in like," Meghan mutters once they're out of earshot. She drains the last of her apple cider.

"Yeah, he's really into Artie." I sip my drink, but it's gone cold.

"Artie? Devon likes *you*."

"Oh, please." I shift on the stone step uncomfortably. My heart is flailing madly like a squirrel in a trap, and my brain is going: *Ohmigoshcouldsheberight?ButMeghanisnuts!But ohmigoshshemayberight!*

"It's obvious," Meghan replies. "Nobody's *that* into cupcakes."

I look up the street, where Artie and Devon are peering into a store window. He taps her on the shoulder and she smiles up at him. *Did that mean anything?* I wonder. *Artie thinks he likes her . . . but maybe he doesn't.*

My heart throbs like a bruise.

"So, what? I should try to steal my ex–best friend's boyfriend?"

"He isn't her boyfriend," Meghan replies. "That's obvious. You can't steal something that doesn't exist."

I press my lips together. This is making me feel weird. I'm not the kind of girl that guys crush out over. And I'm also not the kind of girl who stabs a friend in the back.

But what about an Ex-Best?

I feel awful for even thinking it. But how could I *not* think it?

Too late, anyway: It's already been thought.

I take another swig of my cider, but it tastes horrible to me now.

Confession: Artie and I Have Broken Up Before

Artie and I have been friends since we were toddlers. Her backyard bordered on mine, and we used to play together all the time. We always got along. Not like me and Marco. When he and I were little, we fought like crazy.

People used to say that Artie and I were like sisters. But I have a sister, and it's nothing like being friends with Artie was. Sisters fight. Artie and I never fought. We were more like . . . cousins. Just happy to be together.

But . . . eventually . . . there was a fight.

In third grade. I barely remember what the fight was about. But I do remember how it felt to walk into class and see Artie sitting by someone else. It felt *scary*. It felt like I was in the middle of the ocean, with nothing to hold on to.

Everyone else had their friends. They had things to do after school. They had people to sit with at lunch. I'd never needed them before, but now that I did, I could see that they didn't even realize that I was desperately treading water. They didn't notice that I was alone.

At home, the phone didn't ring. And Marco was out of school that week, which made everything worse.

But Artie — well, it didn't seem like Artie was having the same problems I was. She just sat right down next to Tricia Guererro and struck up a friendship in about five seconds. The next thing I knew, Artie, Tricia, and Jade Jackson were spending all of their time together.

Tread, tread, tread.

I couldn't keep it up. So I called up Artie and apologized.

I expected her to say that she was sorry, too. That she'd missed me. But she didn't. Still, the next day, she showed up at my house after breakfast so that we could walk to school together.

We sat beside each other in class.

I ate lunch with Artie, Tricia, and Jade.

Things returned to normal, more or less.

But, like I said, we were never like sisters. Sisters are for life.

This time, I think the ship is really gone.

Over Sharing

"He's reading it!" Meghan says as she comes up for a sit-up. I glance over at the bleachers, and she pops up again. "Don't look over there!" Back down.

We're in the gym, taking the state-mandated fitness test. Well, Meghan is taking it. I'm holding her legs. She does another sit-up. Another fifty seconds of this, and we'll change places. The boys have already finished their sit-ups and are sitting on the bleachers, watching.

"Ten," she says as she comes up again.

"That was eight," I correct her.

"He's still reading it!" She pops up again. "Twelve. Ugh! I despise sit-ups! Can you tell if he's smiling?"

I nonchalantly look over at the bleachers, where Ben Habib is reading a note. "I can't believe you actually gave him that letter," I tell Meghan. "And I can't believe he's reading it *here*."

Meghan's bangs aren't green anymore. She dyed them bright pink, and right now they are plastered across her sweaty face. "It's so romantic!" she coos, then grunts. "Urgh."

Right. Romantic. We are wearing the required gym uniform — blue-and-white-striped shirts and navy shorts. Polyester. Our gym smells like gladiator sweat and a bucket of dirty disinfectant water. Isn't that a romantic place to read a love note?

Oh, right: *No*.

The coach calls time, and now it's my turn to do sit-ups. We change places, which gives Meghan plenty of time to narrate the rest of Ben's reactions to her secret-admirer note.

"He's folding it up," she says as I crunch my abdominal muscles. "He's putting it back in his backpack. Hayley, he's *saving* it!"

"How many sit-ups is that?" I ask the next time I'm upright.

"Oh, jeez, I have no idea," Meghan admits. "Five?"

It's eight. I roll my eyes. For someone who's a genius nerd, Meghan isn't too good at counting sit-ups.

"I'm going to write him another one," Meghan gushes as I crunch away.

"Bad idea," I grunt.

"Bad?" Meghan smiles, like I'm teasing her. "Are you kidding? The first one worked out; now it's time to go bigger!"

I'm not so sure this is a good idea. Ben is shy. He may get overwhelmed by too much romance.

"Maybe I'll write some poetry," Meghan is saying. "Or make him something. A painting . . ."

The whistle blows, and I roll over onto my side, my stomach muscles aching. "Why don't you wait awhile?" I suggest as everyone gets to their feet.

" 'You never know what is enough unless you know what is more than enough.' " Meghan's round pink face is positively glowing.

"Did you get that off a bumper sticker?"

"It's William Blake!" Meghan grabs my arm and we start toward the locker room. "The English poet. And yes — it's on my neighbor's Corolla. But that doesn't mean it isn't true!"

"Why don't you send your letter to William Blake?" I suggest.

I'm joking, but Meghan rolls her eyes. "He's been dead for about two hundred years."

Well, then, you won't have to worry about embarrassing yourself, I think, but before I can say anything, Marco comes up to us.

"Hey, Hayley, I was just wondering —" He casts a sideways glance at Meghan, then angles his body so that she's behind him. "Um — could I look at your math homework again?"

"Sure, Marco," I tell him. "I'll give it to you after I change."

"Thanks." *He's more than just grateful,* I realize when I see his smile, *he's relieved.* For a moment, I have a flash of what it feels like to deal with Mr. Carter every day. It feels horrible.

Meghan doesn't say anything as we make our way to the locker room. But I feel like I need to offer some kind of explanation, anyway. "He has a lot of trouble with math," I say.

Meghan shrugs. "Then he should do the homework." She pulls open the door to the locker room.

"He tries; he just needs help." I keep my voice down, since the locker room is so echoey.

"Okay," she says, but the way she says it makes it sound like it isn't okay, not really, and suddenly I'm annoyed. Who is Meghan to judge? Marco and I have been friends for years. "You don't know what his life is like," I snap.

"What's it like?" Meghan asks as she sits down on the bench and kicks off her shoes.

The question hits me like a slap. What's Marco's life like? "His parents are . . ." I'm not sure what to call it. ". . . strange. And his sister is autistic. Like, *very* autistic." I don't want to say more. I nibble my pinkie nail as our classmates mill around us, everyone trying to get changed while never letting anyone see their bodies. Half of them probably have an ear out for stray gossip. It stinks worse in here than it does in the gym. It's not a place you can really talk. "It's not a big deal, Meg," I say at last. "What's one homework assignment? It'll help him."

Slowly, Meghan pulls her fresh clothes out of her locker. "Are you sure that you're really helping him?"

I picture Mr. Carter's sneer. "Yes."

She looks right at me with her straightforward blue eyes. "Okay, Hayley," she says.

Okay, I tell myself. *Okay.*

But my hands are shaking as I pull off my socks, and I don't even know why.

Switch

$\mathcal{C}$hloe and I are downstairs in the café, ready, when Dad pulls up on Saturday morning. I'm wearing jeans and my hiking boots, and I have a backpack with water, a few granola bars, and — naturally — three cupcakes. We're going for a hike, so of course I had to bring a few snacks. You can't hike without snacks.

Chloe jumps out of her chair the moment she sees Dad's car. "Bye, Gran!" she shouts, heading for the door.

"Tell your father that I said hello," Gran says to me.

"Okay," I say. Right. *Um, hey, Dad, your ex-mother-in-law says hi!* I'll skip it.

I head out to the sidewalk, where Chloe is giving Dad a huge hug. "Where's Annie?" Chloe asks, peering in the front seat.

"She's going to meet us at the mall," Dad says.

"Mall?" I echo. I look up at the perfect blue sky. "I thought we were going hiking."

Dad cocks his head, as if this is the first he's hearing of it. "Annie wanted to help you girls pick out something to wear for Thanksgiving."

"But . . . last week we talked about what we wanted to do and —" I have to fight to keep the tears from rising to my eyes. I wanted to go hiking with my dad and Chloe, not shopping with Annie.

"I'm sorry, Hayley. I didn't realize you thought that was a definite plan. But now I've told Annie to meet us."

"I don't mind," Chloe chirps. "This'll be fun!"

I sigh and feel like a jerk for complaining. If Chloe doesn't mind going to the mall, then I am definitely not going to make a big stink about it. Even if it is probably the last nice weekend before winter hits us with a frigid slap.

Annie meets us in the cosmetics section of a big department store. She's spraying something from a purple glass bottle onto a strip of heavy white paper when Chloe rushes up behind her and gives her a huge hug. Annie startles in surprise, then hugs back.

"Chloe, I'm so glad you're here! What do you think of this?" She waves the paper under Chloe's nose.

"Mmmm," Chloe says. "Beautiful!"

"What do you think, Bill?" Annie asks, handing it to my father.

Dad shrugs. "Nice."

Annie sighs. "Men never take fragrance seriously." She smiles at me with perfectly even white teeth. My father's girlfriend is really pretty in an ultrafeminine way — long, glossy black hair, high heels, short skirt, full makeup. "What do you think, Hayley?"

I sniff the card. "Smells like room deodorizer."

"Hayley!" Chloe grabs Annie's arm. "Don't listen to her."

"She's just being honest," Annie says, but she places the card on the counter and leaves it there. "So — should we go look at a few dresses?"

"I think I'll —" Dad gestures vaguely over his shoulder and pulls out his iPhone.

Annie nods, and in a moment, the three of us are heading up the escalator. "I made an appointment with a personal shopper," Annie tells Chloe.

"Oooh," Chloe says.

I shake my head at her. Chloe doesn't care about shopping — but she gets excited about new experiences. I watch her gaze down at the shoppers below as we ride the escalator to the second floor. She's soaking up the beauty of the place — the floral arrangements and elegant displays. I bite my poor thumbnail, wishing that I felt the same way.

A petite blond woman in all black meets us in one of the boutique sections. Her name tag says SHEILA. "I've set up a dressing room for you," Sheila says, smiling at us. "I've selected a few things."

"You've already chosen our clothes for us?" Chloe is excited by this, not alarmed, as I am.

"Just some things to get you started, so you won't have to spend time hunting through the racks," Sheila tells her.

We head into the back of the formal gown boutique and go through a gray door. It takes me a moment to realize we're in some kind of secret dressing room — the kind you can only get into if you're prepared to spend serious money. There are four large well-lit and mirrored dressing rooms opening onto a common area. A table has water bottles and a little basket of packaged cookies and snacks.

Sheila points us to our dressing rooms. "Oh, I love this!" Chloe squeals as she holds a yellow dress against her body.

I look at everything in my dressing room. It's all hideous. And stupid. I pick out a hanger holding a teal dress with a fluted skirt. *Who wears a dress to Thanksgiving dinner?*

In my house, Thanksgiving has always been a dress-down meal. I wear jeans. Chloe wears jeans. Mom wears jeans. Dad used to wear jeans. Gran wears a skirt, but she's Gran. She doesn't wear a *new* skirt.

But that's the past. I know that for sure now.

My heart is heavy as I look at the dresses around me. I sit down on the bench in my dressing room and massage my temples. On the other side of my closed door, I can hear Annie and Chloe complimenting each other on their dresses.

"Come show us something, Hayley!" Annie calls.

"Yeah, let's see!" Chloe chimes in.

I sigh, looking down at my hiking boots. *I guess I can't wear these when I meet Annie's parents.* I look up at the dresses. One of them — a red one — has a rose on the sash. It's made of some kind of gauzy fabric. I decide to try it on, since it's the one that will look the most ridiculous with my boots. Maybe it will make me smile.

I get undressed, step into the delicate red dress, then step back into my untied hiking boots. I don't even look in the mirror before walking through the door.

Chloe gasps when she sees me. "You look amazing!" She's standing there in the yellow dress, which looks adorable on her. She's barefoot, and gives a playful twirl to show how the skirt swirls around her legs.

"That looks nice," I tell her.

Annie is looking at me, finger on her chin. She's wearing a fitted silver dress that I would consider perfect attire for the Academy Awards. With her long black hair and light brown skin, she looks like a movie star. I feel like I'm on one of those makeover shows — and I'm the one being made over. "Would you spin, too, Hayley?" she asks.

I clomp in an awkward circle.

Annie comes over and grabs the dress under my armpits. Normally, I would have slapped her hands away, but I'm too shocked. She heaves it up, then stands back. "That's a perfect fit," she says. "And the color really makes your skin glow."

"It's *lovely*," Chloe gushes.

It's ug-lee, I want to tell them. *It has a fake flower on it!* "I don't think it's really me."

"Okay — go try on something else!" Chloe says.

"Those dresses really aren't my style," I confess.

"You're welcome to go look on the racks for something else," Annie says.

"I don't really want to —"

Chloe looks at me eagerly. "You should get this one, Hayley, it looks —"

"I said no!" I snap.

The dressing room is silent. I become aware of the elevator music being piped in over the speakers as I see the tears rise in Chloe's eyes. I want to apologize, but Sheila chooses this moment to walk in. "Well, everyone, how are we doing?" she asks. "Oh, Chloe, that dress is wonderful on you."

"Thank you," Chloe says politely, but all of the joy has drained out of her.

"Chlo, I'm sorry —" I say, but my sister has already retreated into her dressing room.

"And how are you doing?" Sheila asks me. She gives me the up-and-down once-over. "I love that color on you."

I exchange glances with Annie. She folds her arms awkwardly and looks down at her shoes. I feel sorry for her, and sorry for myself, and angry at her, and angry at myself, and I don't know what to do because I don't want this fancy Thanksgiving dinner. I just want my normal life. That's all.

I bite my lip. "I'll take this one," I tell Sheila.

"Wonderful!" Sheila looks like I've made her day.

Well, I guess that makes one of us.

Sandwiched

"Is that going to be enough?" Annie asks, eyeing my sandwich. "Do you want some chips or something?"

"Okay. Thank you." Annie hands me a bag, and we exchange awkward smiles. We're being extra polite to each other after my dressing-room outburst.

Dad pays for everything, and we head out into the food court with our trays.

My sandwich looks a little sad, sitting there on my plate. The top piece of bread is askew and some lettuce is spilling out. I could have made a better-looking sandwich in my own kitchen. But it doesn't taste bad.

Annie and I are quiet as we eat, but Chloe and Dad are talking about a movie they both want to see. Chloe and Dad both love action comedies. So do I. Chloe says, "Should we see it? It's playing in an hour." The movie theaters are next to the food court. Why not?

"Sure," I say, trying hard to sound excited. The red dress is in a bag at my feet, and I wonder how I'm ever going to get myself to wear it.

Chloe reaches for one of my potato chips, and when she pulls her hand back, she manages to knock over her own drink. Apple juice sloshes all over the table and onto Annie's feet.

"Oh, I'm so sorry!" Chloe cries.

Annie's first reflex is to go for the bags. She grabs them off the floor and holds them aloft as Chloe dabs the table with her flimsy napkin. It's about as useful as a Kleenex would be for mopping up a tsunami.

"I'll get more." I dash to the counter, and just as I'm heading back with a huge brick of napkins, I spot my mom.

Happiness flashes through me, and I'm about to call out, when I realize where I am and who I'm with. It would be a complete horrorburger if Mom came over to our table. In an instant, I visualize Dad introducing Mom to Annie. I can hear Annie's nervous giggles and see Mom's brave smile.

Must. Not. Happen.

I turn my back on my mother and scoot back to our table.

"Quick," Dad says, grabbing the napkins from my hands.

Annie dabs at her shoes, which are suede, and I'm wondering how many pairs we will manage to ruin before she decides that it's not worth hanging out with us anymore.

I wipe off my side of the table, and sneak a glance over at Mom's table. Someone sits down across from her.

Oh.

Em.

Gee.

It's Police Officer Ramon! This is . . . what is this? Is she on a *date*?

Make me disappear, I beg silently, just as Mom looks up at me. I see her face register the situation — Chloe apologizing profusely as Dad and Annie scramble to dry the table.

The wet napkins are heavy in my hand and I feel this moment driving us both forward. . . . Now Mom will meet Dad's girlfriend; Dad will meet Mom's date. . . .

And then Mom looks away.

She looks away, like she didn't even see me. *Maybe she didn't,* I think. But I know she did.

My mother can't deal with this situation. Neither one of us can, and — for some reason — I'm angry with her, but also relieved and disappointed in her all at once.

"Hayley, more napkins?" Dad asks, and I snap back to the moment. "Here," I say, handing him some. We get the table cleaned up, and Dad offers to buy Chloe a new sandwich (hers drowned in the apple-juice flood) but she says she was finished, anyway.

"So, should we head to the movie?" Chloe asks.

For a moment, I'm afraid that maybe Mom will turn up in the same movie. But when I look over at her table, I realize that she and Officer Ramon have disappeared.

I wonder what she told him.

Confession:
It's Worse Than You Think

I don't want Mom to meet Annie. The truth is, I don't even want Mom to *see* Annie. Like, ever.

That's because I don't want Mom to realize that she's seen Annie before.

She came to our house once, back when we used to live in a house, before we moved in with Gran.

About a year before Dad moved out, he dumped his low-paying job at the DA's office to work for a glamorous law firm. Annie is a paralegal at the firm. She was a paralegal back then, too.

I remember coming home to find Dad and a beautiful young woman sitting at the dining table. Both were drinking from mugs and laughing over something one of them had said. I walked in, and the moment I saw Annie, my stomach dropped. I didn't know why. I'd never had that reaction to a stranger before.

Dad introduced me to Annie. She tried to be friendly, but I made an excuse and left. I guess they were working on a case. I never asked.

Over a year later, Dad introduced me to his new girl-friend, Annie.

I never mentioned that we had already met.

Maybe Dad has forgotten that Annie came over. Maybe Annie forgot, too. But I think that they're just hoping that *I've* forgotten. After all, it was just for a couple of minutes more than a year ago.

I don't even know if Mom would remember Annie. I guess I just never wanted to take that chance. I don't know what she would think of it.

I don't know what *I* think of it.

But I do know one thing: Mom saw me at a table with Dad, Chloe, and Annie, and Mom didn't say hello. She left.

I'm not sure what to make of that, either.

Questions

"Chlo," I whisper into the darkness. "I'm sorry I snapped at you today."

"When?"

"In the dressing room." Sheesh, has she already forgotten? That's so Chloe.

"It's okay," my little sister says. The room is quiet for a few moments. Chloe and I share a bedroom. We usually lie in our beds and chat for a while before we fall asleep. Suddenly, Chloe asks, "How come you don't like Annie?"

The question lingers between us for a few moments while I try to come up with an answer. Right now, I can't see her face. I wonder what she thinks I'll say. Obviously, I'm not about to tell her that I think Annie may be part of the reason our parents broke up. Or that I think she's Dad's prettier replacement for Mom.

"Why don't you like her?" Chloe repeats.

"I'm asleep," I say at last.

"Come on, Hayley. She's really nice."

"Do I have to like her just because she's nice?"

"Rupert says that you don't like her because you don't want to share our time with Dad."

"Is Rupert my therapist now?" Seriously, I'm starting to think that Chloe's best friend is a little too smart for his own good. Did someone ask his opinion? He's in third grade! What does he know?

"But don't you think that Dad is more fun with Annie around?"

"Not really."

"So Rupert has a point?"

"I don't know."

Chloe sighs, and I stare at the shadowy curtains that turn the red neon from the tattoo place across the street into a rosy pink.

"I like Annie," Chloe whispers.

I breathe in. I breathe out.

The truth is, I like Annie, too. I mean, she isn't someone

I would ever choose as my new best friend. But she is nice.
And she means well. And she smells good.

But I still don't want her around all the time.

Now I'm mad at Rupert.

Why does he have to be right?

Rehearsal

The last bell of the day has rung and I'm on my way to watch Devon. I mean watch *rehearsal*. Of the school musical. Which Devon happens to be in.

Totally different.

Anyway, as I walk down the hall, I notice that people are smiling and chatting — there's a weird energy in the hallway. I can practically feel the place buzzing, like a giant beehive.

"Silver paper," I overhear Ayesha Miller say.

Alexis Toomey nods and grins. "But who — ?"

A certain pink-haired friend of mine is standing beside the double doors to the auditorium. She's grinning and rubbing her hands together, like an evil genius whose plan is starting to fall into place.

"Stop grinning," I tell her.

"I can't!"

"What did you do?"

She grabs my arm and whispers, "I covered Ben's locker in silver foil!" She giggles and adds, "And stuck red hearts all over it."

"Subtle," I say.

"He nearly fainted when he saw it," Meghan says.

"I'll bet. Does he know it was you?"

"Of course not! Don't be crazy. I just happened to be tying my shoe nearby, so I got to see his reaction."

I look down at her ankle boots. "Those have zippers," I point out.

"Like he was paying attention to my shoes!" Meghan lifts one eyebrow, giving me a *You are so loony* look. "He was too busy trying to pull the hearts off."

"He didn't want people to see it?" That doesn't sound good.

"Of course not — guys get embarrassed about that stuff."

"So — don't you worry that you're going overboard?"

"Overboard is where it's at! Which is where you come in."

"Oh, boy." *This is just like the pumpkin,* I think. *She's trying to talk me into another one of her insane schemes.*

"Don't make that face! Just listen — I want you to make me a special cupcake for Ben. Something that says, 'I'm crazy about you.'"

"How about something that just says, 'I'm crazy'?" I suggest.

Meghan laughs, then gets serious. "I know you think I'm nuts." She puts her palm to her forehead. "Maybe this is all a mistake. Am I nuts?"

I bite my lip. "Not in a bad way. I just . . . I don't know how Ben will take all of this. He seems kind of shy."

"He is. . . . But everyone likes to know that someone thinks they're cool, right?"

"Yeah."

"Wouldn't you love it if someone decorated your locker and sent you secret notes?"

I think this over. "I probably would. But I'm not Ben."

Meghan looks hurt. "You're not going to help me?"

"Meg — what if this doesn't turn out the way you want it to? I mean, he's bound to find out who the secret admirer is eventually. What if he doesn't feel the same way about you?"

Meghan takes a deep breath. She peers down the hall, which has started to clear. "I guess I'll be publicly humiliated." Her finger twirls a strand of her orange hair. "But I still want to do it." She looks at me with those blue eyes.

"Are you sure?"

She smiles and gives a one-shoulder shrug. "Well, I've come this far."

I reach out and take her hand. "Okay," I say at last. "Okay, Meg, I'll make the cupcake."

Meghan squeezes my hand, and she's so happy that I know for sure that I've made the right decision. This isn't like the pumpkin at all.

It may be a bad idea . . . but what good is a friend if she won't get behind your bad ideas?

Pop

The front few rows of the auditorium are taken up with backpacks and lounging theater types who are playing cards and waiting for cues. Ms. Lang, the drama teacher and director, sits near the front, too, so I slip into a seat near the back to watch.

Artie and Devon are onstage. I watch for a while, trying to figure out what the scene is about. I can't really tell. For one thing, Devon is using this accent that makes half of his words unintelligible. Also, I'm not even sure whether the accent is supposed to be British or Russian. He kind of just sounds like he's taken too much cough syrup. Still, I can tell he's a really good actor. He seems so *involved* in the scene. And when Artie bats her eyes at him and says, "Until tomorrow, then," I feel a little sick. She watches him leave the stage, and the glance between them lingers.

Mr. Collins, the music teacher, starts pounding away at the piano, and Artie starts to sing. Artie has a big voice, and it fills the auditorium as she launches into the fun, fast number. The musical is something I've never heard of, but it's about a pop star. The songs are catchy — stuff even my mom could hum along to. Artie's song is something I've heard on the radio a thousand times, but with Artie's voice, it has a whole new meaning. It sounds good. Even with the clunky piano as her only accompaniment, it sounds really good.

I look down at my notebook, remembering all of the times I've heard Artie sing. She used to sing in the shower after sleepovers at my house. Or at her house. She would sing in the car.

For years, singing was a private, almost secret thing that Artie did. I was her best friend, so I knew about it. She never, ever wanted to sing in public.

Not until I made her audition for the fall musical.

I look down at my notebook and scribble the word *pop*. Maybe I can make some cupcakes with pop. Or poppy seeds. Pop rocks? This seems like a bad idea, but I write it down, anyway. You never know when a bad idea will somehow turn into a good one. It happens.

"Got anything good?" Devon whispers as he slips into

the seat behind mine. He has to lean forward and his lips are near my ear, which sends a shiver down my spine.

"Not yet," I confess. "Still thinking."

Devon nods, and we finish listening to Artie's song. "What do you think of the play?" he asks when it's over.

"Oh, I love it."

"Can I ask you a question?" I turn to look into his blue gaze. There's a fleck of gold in his right eye, like a beam of sunshine is caught there. "What do you think of my accent?"

I must be hypnotized by that glimmer of gold, because instead of saying something sensible, like, "It's genius," I tell him the truth. "It's kind of hard to understand."

Devon sucks in a deep breath. He drops his head.

"I'm sorry," I say quickly.

"No," he says. He smiles, and then takes my hand. A current travels up the length of my arm, almost like an electric shock. "That's what I thought. It's just — the actor who plays the role in the movie has a Scottish accent. . . ."

"So you want to sound like him?"

"Yes. But it's hard. . . ." Devon shakes his head, and a lock of blond hair tumbles across his eyes. "Ms. Lang says to keep trying. . . ."

"It must make it hard to sing."

Devon looks at me for a long moment. "It really does."

My heart stutters in my chest and I feel that look of his — almost like the one he gave Artie before, in the scene. Except, in that moment, he was acting. And now . . .

The silence between us drags on. Finally, I say, "I think you should just try using your own voice."

"That's just what I needed to hear." He presses my fingers and I feel as if my whole body has gone numb — everything except for my hand and arm, which are alive, crackling with energy.

"Hi, guys! What's up?" Artie stands beside Devon, and he drops my hand.

"Artemis — Hayley and I were just discussing cupcake ideas," he says.

Artie doesn't even look at me. "You're in the next scene, Devon."

"Okay." He flashes me one last grateful look. "Thanks for your honesty, Hayley."

"You're welcome," I whisper as Artie glares. She trails after him toward the stage for a moment, then turns and lopes back toward me. She's smiling, so I smile back. I figure she's going to thank me for making cupcakes for the play, or something, but instead she leans close to me and hisses, "Stay away from my boyfriend."

A cold dagger stabs through me as she leans back, still smiling. For a moment, I think I've misheard her. Then her eyes narrow.

There are so many things I want to say, and they all come rushing into my head at once: *Are you sure he's your boyfriend?* and *What do you think I'm going to do?* and *Are you threatening me?* But before I can say anything, she turns and walks away.

I look down at my hand, which is sitting in my lap.

The hand Devon held.

Suddenly, I feel a little sorry for Artie.

Music

The arts wing is nearly deserted as I leave the auditorium. The hallway is eerily quiet — so quiet that I become extremely aware of the noise my shoes make as the rubber soles squeak across the marble floor. My head is still swirling with thoughts about cupcakes and Artie and Devon when I round the corner and hear a soft rain of musical notes echoing down the hall, reverberating off the metal lockers.

They grow louder as I near the end of the hall and come to the practice rooms. The rooms are soundproof, but someone has left a door open and is playing something soft and sweet on a piano. I used to take piano lessons back when we could afford them, but I was never very good. This, to me, sounds a bit like Brahms or maybe Mozart. It's soothing.

I peek in, and see a curly blond head bowed over the keyboard. "Kyle?"

He stops short and turns to face me. His eyes are blank, but he's wearing a half smile, as if expecting a happy surprise.

"Don't stop. It's just me, Hayley."

"Oh, Fred!" Kyle beams, exposing the dimple in his right cheek. Kyle is blind, by the way. His nickname for me goes back to an incident in fourth grade. I was wearing a vintage bowling shirt with the name *Fred* embroidered over the pocket. I didn't realize Kyle couldn't see, and I was baffled about why he couldn't read my shirt. It was major humiliation for me, but Kyle actually thought the whole thing was funny. "Come on in."

I hesitate in the doorway. "I didn't know you could play the piano."

Kyle turns back to the keys and plays a dramatic *Ta-da!* chord. "Don't you know blind guys love the piano? Stevie Wonder, Ray Charles . . ."

"Art Tatum," I say.

"Whoa! Guess who knows her jazz piano, everyone!" Kyle crows. "Do you play?"

"Just . . . badly." I sit down beside him on the piano bench.

"Hmm." Kyle shrugs. Then he starts to play the familiar *bom-a-did-ah, bom-a-did-ah* that makes up the bottom half of "Heart and Soul." "Show me what you got," he teases.

So I come in with *plink-plink-plink*, and soon we're playing together. "Anyone can play this song."

"But not anyone can make it sound *this* amazing," Kyle counters, and he turns his part into an elaborate riff. "So, Hayley, why so down?"

"You can hear that in my voice?" I take my hands off the keys.

"I can hear it in your fingertips, when you play," he says. "And yeah, your voice. What's up?"

I heave a sigh. "I don't know. Artie and I — We're not getting along."

The dramatic opening to Beethoven's Fifth: *Dunh-dunh-dunh-dun.*

"Thanks, Kyle."

"Sorry. What happened?"

"Nothing, exactly." This isn't quite true, but Kyle doesn't press for more info.

"Is it going to blow over?"

"I doubt it. . . . It isn't really like weather. It feels more like . . . plate tectonics."

"The earth is shifting beneath your feet. Sending up new continents."

"Creating oceans." I toy with the topmost key, making it *plink* over and over. "And meanwhile, I've promised to come up with some brilliant new cupcake that the drama club can sell as a fund-raiser."

"So — what's the cupcake?"

"I don't know. I mean, the musical is about a pop star, so I was thinking maybe . . . poppy seed?" I wince as the words come out of my mouth.

Kyle lifts an eyebrow. "Eeew."

"Pop rocks? Lollipops?"

"Stop, Hayley, you're grossing me out."

"Me, too," I admit.

Kyle laughs. *His dimple is kind of cute,* I realize. *And his eyes are a beautiful shade of gray.* It's interesting to sit near a blind person. You can really study their face without embarrassing yourself. Kyle's skin is pale, but his cheeks are ruddy. He looks like the kind of person who would blush easily, if that were his personality. "So . . . pop. Hey, what about those things — cake pops? Like, a cupcake on a stick?"

"Kyle — you're a genius!"

"So true."

"Don't make me take it back."

"Okay. Besides — I'm not that much of a genius. I didn't help you with the Artie thing."

I blow out a sigh. "Some things can't be helped."

We sit there for a few moments, just being quiet. After a while, Kyle reaches out to the keyboard. *Bom-a-did-ah, bom-a-did-ah* . . .

He pauses and faces me with his eyebrows raised, as if he's asking me a question.

Plink-plink-plink, I play.

Kyle grins. We play "Heart and Soul" together for a while. By the time we finish, I'm smiling again.

There's a lot I don't know about Kyle, but I know he always makes me smile.

Confession: I Didn't Tell Kyle the Whole Truth

The true parts:

Artie and I aren't getting along.

It isn't going to blow over.

I have to make some cupcakes to sell as a fund-raiser.

But none of that is what was on my mind. No, what I was really thinking about is the fact that Meghan is right: Devon definitely doesn't really seem that interested in Artie.

He does when they're onstage, but off it? Hardly. Honestly, he seems more interested in *me*.

And Artie really isn't my friend anymore. We're practically borderline enemies.

So what does that mean?

There's no rule that you can't go for your enemy's crush, right?

I mean — right?

Fractions

I plop down next to Marco on the bus. I don't even bother scanning for Artie anymore. She's there, in the back row. I can hear the familiar tones of her laugh.

"Hey," I say softly.

Marco doesn't look up from his notebook. It's like he's surrounded by a clear bubble of silence.

I stare out the window, watching the stores zip by. It's a gray day, and a low mist hangs over everything. It's probably beautiful out in my old neighborhood. There's a farm near my old house, and on days like this, you could just make out the cows in the blanket of fog. But here, in the town, it just feels damp on your eyelashes, and chill.

Marco sighs, like he's feeling the same way I am. He must feel my glance as I peek onto the open page of his book, because he says, "Carter."

More math. We've moved on to fractions.

"Does this make sense to you?" he demands, almost accusingly. "If I'm dividing 3 by 2/4, shouldn't the answer be 1-1/2? I'm dividing it in half, right?"

"No — first off, you need to make this three into a fraction. 3 over 1. Then you to flip the second fraction. . . ." I go over what Mr. Carter told us the day before.

"But that doesn't make sense," Marco insists.

"Well, it does when you think about it."

"No, it doesn't." Marco's dark eyes flash, but I know he isn't angry with me.

"Look," I say, pulling out my homework. "All you have to know is that division is flipped. Don't worry about it making sense. Just do it. After a while, you'll get it." Chewing the inside of his cheek, Marco stares down at the second problem. "Just be sure to go through all of the steps."

"I always forget to simplify the fractions," Marco admits. "It's points off for that." His finger traces the work in my notebook. "I see . . ." I watch his face. It's almost like watching a candle sputter into flame, then flicker, as if it can't decide whether to catch or go out.

We work on two more problems before the bus lurches up in front of the school. "Thanks, Hayley," Marco says as he shoves his book into his backpack.

"You'll get it," I tell him.

"It's just . . ." Marco looks over his shoulder. The aisle between seats is jammed, but nobody is listening. Everyone is busy shouting and shoving their way to the front. "It's just that if my math grade falls below a C+, they're going to kick me off the soccer team."

"Why? That's totally unfair!"

"I know — and it's almost like Carter wants it to happen. He already met with Coach Klein."

"I *hate* him." I really mean it. Mr. Carter should be fired.

Marco just sighs. The bus has emptied out, so I step into the aisle. Marco scoots out awkwardly, following me. We make our way off the bus, then start to walk toward the school. Our pace is evenly matched — we both like to walk fast.

Once we get to the double doors, Marco says, "I guess I'll see you later, Hayley."

"Marco, wait —" I pull my notebook from my backpack and shove it at him. "Make sure you finish the homework."

Marco hesitates. "I can't ask you again."

"You don't have to ask," I tell him. I swat him in the arm with the notebook.

"Okay." Marco looks me in the eye. "I'll keep up with the homework from now on. I swear."

"I know you're doing your best," I tell him.

He shrugs, taking the notebook. "I hope it's enough." He gives me another sad smile, then turns to walk away.

King Kong Cupcakes
(Banana-Coconut-Macadamia-Nut Cupcakes)
(makes approximately 12 cupcakes)

I basically tweaked the Rain Forest Cupcakes and added Chocolate-Coconut Frosting. Bananas. Nuts. Perfect for Meghan.

INGREDIENTS:

- 1 medium very ripe banana, mashed well
- 2/3 cup coconut milk
- 1 teaspoon coconut extract
- 1/2 teaspoon vanilla extract
- 1/2 cup granulated sugar
- 1/4 cup brown sugar
- 1/3 cup canola oil
- 1-1/4 cups gluten-free, all-purpose flour, such as Bob's Red Mill
- 1 teaspoon baking powder
- 1/4 teaspoon baking soda
- 1/2 teaspoon salt
- 1/2 cup chopped toasted macadamia nuts

INSTRUCTIONS:

1. Preheat the oven to 350°F. Line a muffin pan with cupcake liners.
2. In a small bowl, whisk together the banana, coconut milk, coconut extract, vanilla extract, granulated sugar, brown sugar, and oil.
3. In a larger bowl, sift together the gluten-free flour, baking powder, baking soda, and salt, and mix.
4. Add the dry ingredients to the wet ones a little bit at a time, and combine using a whisk or handheld mixer, stopping to scrape the sides of the bowl a few times, until no lumps remain. Add the chopped macadamia nuts and combine completely.
5. Fill cupcake liners two-thirds of the way and bake for 18–22 minutes. Transfer to a cooling rack, and let cool completely before frosting.

Chocolate-Coconut Frosting

INGREDIENTS:

    1/2 cup margarine

    1/2 cup cocoa powder

    1 teaspoon coconut extract

    2-1/2 cups confectioners' sugar

    3 tablespoons coconut milk

INSTRUCTIONS:

1. In a bowl, using a handheld mixer, cream the margarine. Sift in the cocoa powder and mix with the margarine until completely combined.

2. Add the coconut extract and then start beating in the confectioners' sugar in 1/2-cup intervals, adding a little of the coconut milk in between batches. Continue to beat the frosting until it is light and fluffy, about 3–7 minutes.

Salt

$\mathcal{M}$om is sitting at a table in the café, chatting with Police Officer Ramon.

Awk-ward.

I really want to talk to her about Marco and Meghan and Devon and Artie. But she's busy . . . smiling. Smiling and smiling at Ramon, who is smiling and smiling at her. I just wish they'd stop *smiling* so much.

Which brings me to my next subject: I wish I had someone to talk to about my mother and Ramon.

But who am I going to call? Meghan? We weren't friends when my parents got divorced, and she doesn't really know the whole history. Besides, I don't want *advice*. I just want someone to listen. And Meghan is really more of an advice girl. Three weeks ago, I would've called Artie. But that's out. And Marco — forget it. He's got too much going on to hear me. My sister is sitting nearby, but she's with Rupert, and I don't want more free psychoanalysis. Besides, Chloe probably thinks Officer Ramon is great. Just like Annie is great. Everyone's great!

I wish I could feel that way.

I tap in the cocoa and mix it carefully into the rest of the batter. Then I add a generous amount of sea salt. It's almost like I'm adding the tears that are hidden behind my eyes, the ones I can't seem to shed for some reason.

I've been thinking about Marco all afternoon. Not just about the trouble he's having in Mr. Carter's class, but just about how hard things have been for him in general. I wish our friendship was like it used to be — easy. Automatic. Almost thoughtless.

I feel the same way about Artie. I wish I'd never realized she was awful. It was so much easier.

In books or movies, whenever a friendship ends, the friends just become enemies. And then the heroine makes perfect new friends who solve all of her problems. Instead, I've got a still-kind-of friend who needs my help, an ex-friend who isn't quite an enemy, and a new friend who's bossy and maybe halfway nuts. Fun, but nuts.

Nuts. A thought strikes me: *Maybe nuts are what's needed.*

I decide to add a few pecans to the recipe.

"You seem lost in thought," says a voice behind me.

Turning, I see the warm, smiling face of Mr. Malik. He's peeking out from behind a tall bouquet of dahlias. "I didn't hear you come in."

He places the weekly bouquet — a barter arrangement from his flower shop — on the counter and takes a seat. "You were lost in thought," he says in his elegant Pakistani accent.

"Thinking about friends," I tell him as I scoop batter into paper cupcake liners.

"Good friends?"

"Old friends. Ex-friends, maybe." I shrug.

"They're hard to replace." Mr. Malik places his fingertips together.

"Yeah."

"It's hard to compare someone you've known your whole life to someone you've known only a few weeks," he says, and I nearly fall on the floor because that is exactly the problem and I hadn't been able to figure out how to say it until he just did.

He sighs and smiles at the same time. "I remember how I felt when my wife died," he says. "I lost my closest friend, and I did not want to know anyone else. All I wanted was her. But, eventually, I made new friends. And, in time, those friends that I had known for a few weeks became friends that I have known for years. And I treasure them, and the memories we have made together."

"Mr. Malik! There you are. Just in time for tea and madeleines." Gran bustles out from the back room, smiling. Mr. Malik brightens at the sight of her as she pours hot water into the teapot and takes a plate of cookies to a small table near the window.

"Will you excuse me?" Mr. Malik asks. "It's time for me to have tea . . . with my friend." He gives me a courtly bow.

"Sure," I tell him. I want to say thanks, too, but I'm worried it will sound weird, so I try to just look grateful for what he's said. I watch as he goes to sit down with my grandmother, who never would have become his close friend if his wife hadn't passed away. That was sad. It was tragic — but something good still came out of it.

Chloe and Rupert sit near Gran, playing some card game that Chloe has invented. That is another friendship that grew out of a sad story. Chloe's friends turned on her and started bullying her. For a long time, Chloe's only companion was her imaginary friend, Horatio. But she changed schools and met Rupert. And he understood her in a way that her old friends never did.

Mom laughs at something Ramon has said. She catches my eye and waves to me. I wave back, and Ramon nods. Pressing my lips together, I turn back to my cupcakes.

I guess Ramon is my mother's new friend. The person who appeared to fill the hole my father created when he left.

It's funny to think that my mom might be feeling kind of the same way that I'm feeling — deserted. Confused. Relieved to have a new friend.

I guess I should be glad for my mom.

Maybe I will feel that way.

In the future.

Invite

I'm sitting at dinner that night, minding my own business, when Chloe asks, "Can we invite Ramon to Thanksgiving dinner?"

Suddenly, it's like I don't know what to do with the bite of fish in my mouth. I can't seem to swallow it. I just chew and chew and chew until it's practically fish juice, and then I'm still chewing and I have to take a sip of water to wash it down.

Gran watches Mom, a little smile on her lips, as if she's wondering how my mother will respond. Mom looks dazed. She gazes off toward the kitchen, as if she's considering trying to escape.

"Isn't he your boyfriend?" Chloe asks. Her face turns pink, and I think she's realized that she has said something embarrassing.

"He isn't my boyfriend," Mom says in a tone of voice that means, "not *exactly*."

"Okay, well, even if he's just a friend, can't he come over?" Chloe asks. "Don't you remember that he said he spends Thanksgiving alone?"

"He spends it at a soup kitchen," I correct her. "Maybe he likes helping people."

"We're having dinner early," Chloe points out. "He'll still have time to go to the soup kitchen. Right, Gran?"

"Hmm. Hayley, dear, please pass the salt," Gran says.

Mom looks at me, as if she knows that I'm the one who will say no. "Can't we just keep Thanksgiving small?" I beg.

"Chloe, sweetheart," Mom says to my sister, "Thanksgiving is really about family."

"But Hayley and I are having Thanksgiving with Annie and her parents, and they aren't family," Chloe insists.

I drop my fork onto my plate and put my head in my hands.

"You're having Thanksgiving with Annie's family?" Mom asks.

"You didn't know that?" Chloe's mouth is a tiny O. She looks at me in horror, but I just shake my head.

"Well, this is interesting." Gran stands up suddenly. "I think I'll have a glass of wine."

"Your father told me that he wanted to spend Thanksgiving with you girls," Mom says. "He didn't say anything else. Is —" She turns to look at me. "Are Annie and your father engaged?"

"No, of course not," I say, and the moment the words are past my lips, I wonder if it's true. Are they? I mean, Chloe and I are going all the way to Connecticut to meet Annie's parents on Thanksgiving. That seems like . . . well, maybe it could be something.

Something big.

Mom's eyes sparkle, and I realize that tears have sprung into them. This stabs me like a stake in the heart. I take her hand just as Gran returns to the dining room with a glass of white wine. "Well!" Gran says brightly as she settles into her chair.

"Please, Mom?" Chloe pleads. "Please can't we just invite Ramon?"

"Why is it such a big deal, Chloe?" I ask.

"Because I don't want him to spend Thanksgiving by himself," she says. Her eyes are wide and innocent, and I want to hug her and throttle her all at once.

Mom puts up a hand. She blinks twice, then nods. "Okay, Chloe. We'll invite him."

"Well, that will be lovely," Gran says.

Chloe looks relieved, then flashes me a nervous smile.

I look away. "May I be excused?"

"Sure, Hayley."

Great. *May I be excused from Thanksgiving, too?*

Confession: My Mom Never Cries

I remember the day my dad moved out. I watched from the window in my room as my father helped two moving men haul things to the van. It didn't take that long — less than an hour.

Finally, the men closed the door on the back of the van and drove away. There were still a few small things Dad wanted to take with him, so Mom actually helped him carry a couple of the boxes out to his car.

She didn't cry.

She didn't cry when she was laid off from the job she loved.

On the day we packed up the rest of our things to move out of our home, Mom was busy labeling boxes and color-coding a chart so we would know where everything went. She didn't cry then, either.

The only time I've ever seen Mom cry is the time that Chloe fell off the swing face-first. She was three years old and had been lying on her stomach, swinging back and forth. When she fell, she went tumbling head over heels and cut her forehead on a rock. Even then, Mom was calm. She held a handkerchief to Chloe's head and dialed 911 on her cell phone with the other hand. Mom soothed Chloe all the way to the hospital. It was only later, after the doctor put seven stitches in Chloe's forehead, after we went home and Mom tucked Chloe into bed, it was only after all of that that I went downstairs for a drink of water and heard Mom telling Dad all about what had happened, and sobbing like she couldn't stop. She told him that she had been frightened and that she blamed herself for letting Chloe swing on her stomach. I heard my father comforting her as I turned and tiptoed away.

That was the only time I ever saw her cry. That, and tonight, at the table, when she asked if Dad and Annie were engaged. I mean, she didn't lose it and start boo-hooing, but I saw tears in her eyes. Then she blinked, and they disappeared.

It made me remember the night of Chloe's accident, when Mom hid her tears from both of us. And I realized something: It isn't that Mom never cries.

It's just that she never lets us see.

Bananas

"Hayley!" I hear Meghan shouting as I make my way toward homeroom. "Hayley!" She hurries up behind me and grabs my elbow. She holds up a finger as if to say, "one minute," then takes a deep breath. "I ran too fast," she gasps, then sucks in more air. "Sorry."

"Take your time," I tell her.

Her face is pink as she straightens up and fans herself with her fingers. "Now I'm all sweaty before class." She sniffs her armpit. "I probably smell!"

"You're fine," I tell her.

"Do you have it?" she asks.

I reach into my backpack and pull out a Chinese-food container.

She lets out a whoop. "What flavor?"

"Banana," I tell her, "with chocolate frosting." I had cut out a small paper monkey and written I'M BANANAS FOR YOU on the front. Then I glued it to a toothpick and stuck it in the cupcake. It had come out really cute, if I do say so myself. Which I do.

"It's perfect!" Meghan says, closing the lid back up. "I can't wait to stick it in his desk!" I have to grab her sweater to stop her from dashing away.

"What's up?" she asks.

"Just giving you one more chance to think this over."

"I don't know, Hayley." Meghan runs her hands through her bangs, then balls her hands into fists, so that tufts of pink hair sprout through her fingers like cactus flowers. "I know you think I'm crazy. Sometimes I think I'm not the easiest person to be friends with." Her eyes are large, and together with the hairstyle, she looks like a troll doll. My new friend — she has some challenges.

"You're not the hardest person, either," I say.

"Really?" She combs her fingers through her hair, rearranging the spiky mass.

"You're not even in the top ten," I tell her truthfully. "You just have a lot of ideas and a lot of energy. And sometimes it goes a little —"

"Haywire?"

"Yeah."

"That's what my mom says. She's always like, 'Slow down, Meghan! Think about what you're doing!'"

"So why don't you do that?" I ask.

"Because I never listen to my mom. Besides, if I slowed down, there wouldn't be time to do everything!"

I laugh. "Okay, Meg." There's no point in trying to stop her. So I don't.

Somehow, Meghan manages to wait until we are in math class to surprise Ben with the cupcake.

"Don't you want to see his reaction?" Meghan asks.

I know the right answer. "Um, yes?"

Anyway, so Ben walks into class, and there is the Chinese-food container sitting on top of his desk. Meghan had put sparkly stickers all over it and had written his name on top.

Ben puts his backpack on the ground. Then he pokes at the top of the container with his pen. It's like he's defusing a bomb or something. He manages to lift a flap that way, and when he looks inside, his eyebrows lift. Lifted eyebrows — what does it mean?

I feel like I'm about to pass out. It isn't even *my* love note — not really — but the fact that I can't read his reaction stresses me out. I hear Meghan tapping her fingers on her desk and realize that she's stressed, too.

He lifts the cupcake out of the container and reads the card. He stares out the window for almost a full minute, then he sits down at the desk.

Eat it! I think at him. *Eat the cupcake!*

Finally, he takes a bite. Then another.

My head swims with relief. *He likes it.*

"Hey, Hayley," Marco says as he slips into the desk beside mine. He hands me a folded piece of paper — my homework, which he borrowed on the bus again this morning. He sees me looking at the far corner of the room and looks quickly from Ben's cupcake to my face. He bites his lip and is about to say something when Mr. Carter comes in.

"Everyone take out your homework," he drones. We pass it up. Marco hands his in without looking in my direction.

As all of those papers make their way forward, Meghan passes a note over her shoulder.

OMG, Ben has chocolate cupcake
stuck on his tooth! Gross!

I draw a smiley face with crazy hair sticking up out of it, then hand it back.

She unfolds the paper, then turns and grins at me. I sneak another glance at Ben. He's folding up the wrapper very intently. I think it's interesting that he hasn't looked around the classroom at all. *Doesn't he wonder who sent him the cupcake?* I think. *Or maybe he already knows.* Marco peers over at me again, his face thoughtful.

"All right, everyone, please clear your desks," Mr. Carter announces. "We're going to have a pop quiz."

The class groans, and books slam shut. Mr. Carter gets Tanisha to pass out the quizzes. I sigh as I look at the page. Division of fractions. Fine. I'd rather be taking a pop quiz than listening to Mr. Carter read from the book or pick on Marco.

I'm halfway through the fifth problem when I realize that Marco is having a coughing fit beside me. When I look over, his eyes go wide. *Help,* he mouths.

Help? I look down at his paper. He's only answered one problem. And it's the wrong answer. I feel seasick, as if the room has begun to sway.

I shake my head. *No.*

Marco takes a shaky breath and looks up at the front of the room, where Mr. Carter is looking over the homework. Marco moves on to the next problem.

I try to focus on my paper, but I'm dimly aware that Marco has forgotten to simplify the fractions. That's points off. Besides, it makes the problem harder to solve.

No, I tell myself. *Don't do it.*

But then I imagine an F at the top of Marco's paper. I imagine him getting kicked off the soccer team. And before I know what I'm doing, I clear my throat and Marco looks up.

I don't have to do much. I just sit up straighter, move my arm, tilt my paper, and go back to solving problems. When I finish, I pretend to be going back over my work, so Marco will have time to see everything. But I don't actually check my answers. My ears are buzzing, and I can't concentrate. I'm not even sure who I'm mad at — Marco, or myself.

Both, I guess.

I watch Marco's face as Tanisha picks up the tests. He's smiling, and I realize that he's happy — he's confident. This is probably the first pop quiz in math that he's ever taken where he knows he'll get a good grade. Then Mr. Carter won't be able to say anything.

But I feel like I'm covered in some sort of oozy, slimy goo. Like I'll never get it off. When Marco catches my eye, he blushes. *Sorry,* he mouths.

I press my lips together and stare straight ahead, and I know in that moment that this is the last time. The last time.

It has to be.

I Can Take It

I hear Marco whisper my name as I walk out of Mr. Carter's classroom, but I don't turn around. I walk quickly down the hall, eyes on the floor. I can feel him hurrying after me. I don't want to hear his apologies. I don't want to hear his excuses. I just want to get away.

I turn the corner quickly and run right into Devon. "Hayley!" he says, flashing his brilliant smile.

"Oh, hi."

"You okay?"

He cares. The fact that Devon's eyebrows are scrunching at me in worry makes me feel dizzy. I'm aware that Marco is hovering behind me. Waiting to talk to me, most likely. But I don't really want to talk to him right now. "I'm . . . fine. I'm great, in fact." I try to shake off my gloom and return Devon's glowing smile.

His momentary concern for me passes. "Hey — guess what? I ditched the accent, like you told me to. And Ms. Lang said she liked it better." He grabs my hand and kisses it. "I owe you my thanks, milady," he adds in a goofy English accent.

"Oh, you're welcome." I guess Marco has finally taken the hint, or else he's just bored by my conversation with Devon, because he gives up and moves on. My head swims with relief. "Hey — I, uh, I came up with a fund-raiser idea. How about cake pops? I could do a couple of different flavors —"

"What's a cake pop?"

"Cake on a stick, basically. Like a lollipop. You dip them in frosting —"

"Cake on a stick? I love it!"

"Well, I didn't invent them. . . ." I blush, feeling like an idiot.

"You're a genius for even thinking of them for the fund-raiser."

"Well, actually, Kyle thought of them." *Okay, lips: Stop moving. Silence!*

"Okay, Hayley." Devon's blue eyes sparkle. "You're not a genius. And this idea is just okay. Remind me never to give you a compliment."

I laugh. "I guess I'm not very good at taking them."

Devon's hand reaches toward my face, and I suck in my breath. I feel his fingertips linger in my hair for a moment. My heart slows down. Time freezes.

Devon pulls his fingers away and holds them in front of my face. "You had a piece of fluff in your hair," he says. Then he tosses it away. I watch as the small blue pill from my sweater floats toward the floor.

I feel as if I'm made of wax, like I'm shifting and melting.

Devon smiles a slow, soft smile. "Pretty sweater, by the way," he says. "If you can take the compliment."

"I can take it," I whisper, but he has already stepped past me, continuing on to class.

Confession:
DID YOU JUST SEE THAT???

AAAAAAAAAAAAAAAAAAAAAAAA
IIIIIIIIIIIIIIIIIIIIIIIIIIIIIIIIIIIIIIIIIIIIIIIII
EEEEEEEEEEEEEEEEEEEEEEEEEE
EEEEEEEEEEEEEEEEEEEEEEEEEEE!
!!

Coconut-Macaroon Cake Balls

(makes approximately 80–90 cake balls)

Pop them on a stick or just pop them in your mouth! Cake balls are the perfect bite-sized treat!

INGREDIENTS:
- 1 cup coconut milk
- 1 teaspoon coconut extract
- 1/2 teaspoon vanilla extract
- 3/4 cup granulated sugar
- 1/3 cup canola oil
- 1-1/4 cups all-purpose flour
- 1 teaspoon baking powder
- 1/2 teaspoon baking soda
- 1/2 teaspoon salt
- 1 cup unsweetened shredded coconut flakes, plus more to sprinkle on top
- 1–2 12-ounce bags semisweet or white-chocolate chips (optional)
- Plastic fork or unwanted metal fork (optional)
- Toothpicks or lollipop sticks (optional)

INSTRUCTIONS:

1. Preheat the oven to 350°F. Grease a 9" x 12" baking pan and set aside.

2. In a bowl, stir together the coconut milk, coconut extract, vanilla extract, granulated sugar, and oil.

3. In a larger bowl, sift together the flour, baking powder, baking soda, and salt.

4. Add the dry ingredients to the wet ones a little bit at a time, and combine with a whisk or handheld mixer, stopping to scrape the sides of the bowl a few times, until no lumps remain. Add the coconut flakes and combine completely.

5. Fill the baking pan with the batter, smoothing over with a spatula since the batter will be a little thick, and bake for 18–22 minutes. Transfer to a cooling rack, and let cool completely.

6. Make the white-chocolate frosting as described on page 137. Take the cake you just baked and crumble it into the bowl with the frosting, breaking the cake into very small pieces to make mixing easier.

7. Either with a large spatula or spoon (or wash your hands and dig in!), mix together the cake crumbs and the frosting until completely and thoroughly combined. Chill in the refrigerator for 30 minutes.

8. Line two rimmed baking sheets with wax paper. Remove the cake–frosting mixture from the refrigerator and, with a melon baller or a tablespoon, scoop the mixture onto the baking sheets and roll into balls of about the same size.

9. Chill the cake balls in the refrigerator for at least 4 hours (or overnight), or place in the freezer and freeze them to speed up the process.

10. When the cake balls are firm to the touch, you can store them in a sealed container in the refrigerator and remove them to serve. The next steps are optional.

11. Place the chocolate chips in a microwaveable bowl and heat on 50% power, stirring every 15 seconds, until the chocolate is completely melted and smooth.

12. Take your plastic fork and break off the two

middle tines to make a cake ball dipper (you balance the cake ball in between the two outer fork tines). Alternately, use a toothpick or two, or a spoon. Place wax paper on baking sheets nearby and remove a few cake balls from the refrigerator, leaving the rest to stay cold until ready to be dipped.

13. One at a time, dip the cake balls into the melted chocolate with the fork, rolling it around quickly to completely cover, and then placing on the wax paper to cool and harden. Repeat until all of the cake balls have been covered in chocolate, melting additional chocolate as necessary.

14. If you want, sprinkle a little of the coconut flakes on top of each cake ball, or if you're feeling daring, try to roll the cake ball in coconut flakes to cover completely.

15. Insert a toothpick or lollipop stick about halfway into each cake ball, being careful not to poke through the other end.

16. Leave the cake balls out until the chocolate hardens (about 1 hour), then store in tightly sealed containers in your refrigerator.

White-Chocolate Frosting

INGREDIENTS:

    6 ounces white-chocolate chips

    1/2 cup margarine

    1 teaspoon vanilla extract

    2 cups confectioners' sugar

INSTRUCTIONS:

1. Melt the white-chocolate chips in a small bowl in the microwave, then set aside to cool to room temperature.
2. In a large bowl, using a handheld mixer, cream the margarine until lighter in color. Add the vanilla extract, and then slowly add the confectioners' sugar in 1/2-cup batches, mixing completely before adding more.
3. Add the melted white chocolate and beat on high speed until the frosting becomes light and fluffy, about 3–7 minutes.

Glop

I'm dipping a cake pop in white-chocolate frosting when I hear the bell jingle over the door. This cake-pop thing is harder than it looks. The real trick is getting the frosting to go on evenly. If you can do that, then you're golden. All you have to do is dip the pop into sprinkles or mini-chips, or whatever, and they look great.

But my frosting keeps glopping. Yes, that is the technical term.

I let out a low growl and toss the cake pop into the trash. This is the fifth one I've ruined.

I'm minding the café by myself. Unless you count Rupert and Chloe, who are also here. Rupert is playing the piano, and Chloe is sketching at a table nearby. We have the place to ourselves. Well, we did . . . up until one minute ago.

"Ahem," a voice says behind me. "Uh — anyone home?"

I turn to see Kyle standing at the counter, smiling. "Hey, Kyle," I say. "It's Hayley."

"I figured. I just wasn't sure you were open — it seemed like you were busy." Kyle is legally blind, but he can still make out shadows and shapes.

"I'm here — struggling with frosting."

"Better than struggling with hungry sharks."

"Or rabid monkeys."

"There! Now you have a whole new outlook." He grins, and a lock of curly blond hair falls into his gray eyes.

I wipe my frosting-covered hands on my apron. "Can I get you something?"

"What do you have in the cupcake department?"

"I've got caramel with white-chocolate frosting, banana with chocolate frosting, salty chocolate with chocolate frosting, and lemon with lemon frosting." I make a mental note that we've run out of the pumpkin spice with maple frosting. *Time to bake more*, I think.

"I'll take banana with chocolate," he says. I reach for a square of wax paper and pull out one of the cupcakes. Just as I'm placing it on the plate, Kyle says, "This is the kind you gave Ben, right?"

His voice is so casual that for a moment, I think I've misheard him. "What?"

"Didn't you make one of these for Ben Habib? He told me about it." Kyle hands me a five-dollar bill, like we're just making normal café conversation. Rupert's fingers dance over the keys, and I feel my heart flutter in time to the quick notes of the piano.

I stand there a moment, considering what to say. It probably took Ben about three seconds to figure out where the cupcake came from. Of course. *Dur*, I think. I mean, I'm not the only person on earth who knows how to make cupcakes. But how many people at our school would make a banana one topped with chocolate frosting and a teeny-tiny marzipan banana?

"Am I embarrassing you?" Kyle asks.

"No."

"Because I can't see your face, so I don't know."

"I'm not embarrassed — it's just . . . Yeah, I made the cupcake. But not in that way! It was from . . . someone else."

"Oh."

"But now Ben thinks it's from me?"

"Well, kind of."

Rupert stops playing suddenly, and the room is quiet.

"Would you tell him that it isn't?"

"Sure."

"Because I don't want him to get the wrong idea." *Why am I going on and on about this?*

Kyle smiles. "No problem, Hayley."

For a moment, I wonder why we're still standing there. Then I look down at the five-dollar bill in my hand and remember that I need to make change. "I'll be right back," I say, and head over to the register.

Once I hand Kyle his change, he takes his plate and walks over to the piano, which Rupert has just abandoned. Kyle puts down his plate on top of the piano, then feels the outer edges of the keyboard. He places his fingers at the center and begins to play. It's a piece of music I recognize. Brahms. It's lovely, and seems perfect with the fading late-afternoon light that is streaming through our front windows.

I look over at the trash, where my lumpy cake pop sits atop a pile of napkins and empty paper cups. My frustration has faded away, and I feel ready to try again. Besides, Kyle is right — struggling with frosting is a lot better than struggling with hungry sharks — or other things.

I guess I just needed some perspective. *I'm glad Kyle came in*, I realize. And I'm glad I got to clear up that Ben thing. I didn't want Kyle to think I really was behind all of the insane romantic behavior. I mean, I didn't want *Ben* to think that.

It doesn't really matter what Kyle thinks.

Right?

Gingered Pumpkin Cupcakes
(makes approximately 12 cupcakes)

This is the perfect blend of spice and sweet. Finally, something I can really be thankful for.

INGREDIENTS:

- 1 cup canned pumpkin
- 1/4 cup milk
- 1 teaspoon vanilla extract
- 1 cup brown sugar
- 1/3 cup canola oil
- 1-1/4 cups all-purpose flour
- 1/2 teaspoon baking powder
- 1/2 teaspoon baking soda
- 1 teaspoon ground cinnamon
- 2 teaspoons ground ginger
- 1/4 teaspoon salt
- 1/3 cup diced candied ginger, plus more to sprinkle on top (optional)

INSTRUCTIONS:

1. Preheat the oven to 350°F. Line a muffin pan with cupcake liners.

2. In a large bowl, whisk together the pumpkin, milk, vanilla extract, brown sugar, and oil.
3. In another bowl, sift together the flour, baking powder, baking soda, cinnamon, ground ginger, and salt, and mix.
4. Add the dry ingredients to the wet ones a little bit at a time, and combine using a whisk or handheld mixer, stopping to scrape the sides of the bowl a few times, until no lumps remain. Add the diced candied ginger and combine completely.
5. Fill cupcake liners two-thirds of the way and bake for 22–24 minutes. Transfer to a cooling rack, and let cool completely before frosting.
6. OPTIONAL: Sprinkle additional diced candied ginger on top of the frosted cupcakes.

Ginger Cream-Cheese Frosting

INGREDIENTS:

    1/3 cup cream cheese, softened to room temperature

    1/2 cup margarine or butter, softened to room temperature

    2-1/2 cups confectioners' sugar

    1 teaspoon vanilla extract

    2 teaspoons ground ginger

INSTRUCTIONS:

1. In a bowl, cream together the cream cheese and margarine or butter completely. Slowly add the confectioners' sugar in 1/2-cup batches, mixing completely before adding more.
2. Add the vanilla extract and ground ginger and beat on high speed until the frosting becomes light and fluffy, about 3–7 minutes.

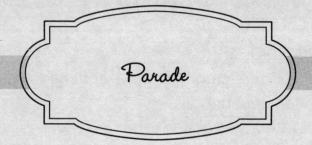

Parade

"The Snoopy balloon — turn it up!" I tell Chloe, who obediently pokes at the remote.

"Who are all of these bands?" my sister asks as another obscure music act lip-synchs atop what looks like a gingerbread boat. "Are they all from some TV station that we don't get?"

"All of the real celebrities are busy celebrating Thanksgiving, like normal people," I tell her.

"Couldn't they get some British bands?" Chloe demands. "They don't celebrate Thanksgiving."

"Well, they should." I spread cream-cheese frosting on top of the gingered pumpkin cupcake I'm holding. It's eleven in the morning, and the house smells amazing. Gran made her famous cinnamon buns, and I've already had two.

"How are we doing?" Mom asks as she walks into the kitchen. "Hayley, honey, those look gorgeous." She reaches toward the cupcake as if she's going to steal a bit of frosting, but I yank it away. "Not until after dinner!"

Mom laughs and hurries off to straighten a fork that has gone askew. Mom set the table in our little apartment last night, and Gran insisted that we use her good china, so everything is gleaming and ready.

The doorbell rings, and Chloe runs to get it. "It's Ramon!" she shouts unnecessarily when she peeks through the peephole. He's the only person we invited, and he's right on time.

Ramon looks surprisingly handsome in black pants and a bright blue button-down shirt. His shoes are shined, and he looks freshly showered. He's carrying a large casserole dish.

"What have you brought us?" Mom asks, taking it from his hands. "It smells wonderful."

"Paella," he replies, smiling warmly.

When Mom lifts the lid of the dish, a spicy aroma makes my stomach growl loud enough for Chloe to say, "Excuse you, Hayley!"

I blush and go back to frosting my cupcake as Gran walks in with a vase of red flowers. She oohs and ahhs over Ramon's paella, and before I know it, dinner is on the table, and we're ready to eat.

It's lunchtime, really, and the meal doesn't look like any Thanksgiving we've ever had before. Gran has cooked salmon, Mom has made kale spiced with garlic and red pepper, and — of course — we have paella. No stuffing. I'm trying not to feel disappointed.

I take a bite of Ramon's dish — and have to admit that it's my favorite thing on the table. It's a spicy mix of sausage, rice, tomatoes, and seafood.

"This is awesome!" Chloe gushes, and I agree.

Ramon tells a story about the time he tried to explain the Macy's Thanksgiving Day Parade to his relatives in Honduras. "They like to tease me because my Spanish isn't perfect. So when I told them that there were giant balloons, they laughed. 'You're saying giant *balloons*!' They thought I must have meant something else. 'You're saying balloons as big as a house!' It took forever for me to convince them that I really meant balloons, after all."

Mom clears away the plates, and I pass out cupcakes while Chloe hands everyone a pale blue piece of paper and a pen.

"What's this?" Ramon asks.

"It's so that you can write down something you're thankful for," Chloe tells him. She looks at me. "We're starting a new tradition."

"I'm thankful that I didn't have to cook a turkey this year," Mom says.

Ramon smiles at her, but it's a faraway smile, as if he's thinking of something else. "I have much to be thankful for," he says, and then he bends his head over his piece of paper, writing something.

"As do we all." Gran smiles at me, and I know instantly that she's thankful that Chloe, Mom, and I came to live with her.

I hear Chloe's pen scratching, and I imagine that she's thankful to have met Rupert. Or to be in a new school.

Mom is writing, too, but I can't imagine what she's thankful for. Is she glad she got divorced? Or is she writing something goopy about Ramon?

I peer down at my blank paper.

I have a lot to be thankful for. I know that. We have a home here with Gran. I get to make cupcakes whenever I like. I found a good friend in Meghan.

But I don't feel like writing any of that.

I'm thankful that this year is ending.

I'm glad it's almost over, that it's rolling away into the past, leaving only the future.

I fold my paper in half and give it to Chloe, who collects the scraps. Then she walks over to the fireplace and tosses them in.

I watch the flame lick the edges of the paper. One of the pieces turns to ash and flutters up the chimney. I like to think that one is mine.

Silence settles over the room, and then — out of the blue — Ramon starts to sing. It's a gentle song in Spanish, so I have no idea what he's saying, but the sounds are sweet and a little sad. He has a lovely voice. Not loud or showy, just nice, and I imagine that he's singing about the year ending and something new beginning.

His face blurs, and I realize that tears are welling in my eyes, threatening to spill down my cheeks. I hide my face in my napkin, then get up to go to the bathroom, where I splash water on my face and look at myself in the mirror. My skin looks pale and blotchy. I look ill, to tell you the truth. I feel queasy.

Happy Thanksgiving, I think.

When I come back into the living room, Rupert is sitting at the table, munching a cupcake. "These are delicious," he tells me.

"Thanks," I reply. "What are you doing here?"

"Hayley!" Chloe squeals.

"I just mean — Rupert, aren't you having Thanksgiving at your own house?"

"Yes, and that's why I'm here. I'm just taking a break from the noise." He rolls his eyes. "It's so nice and quiet here."

Mom and Ramon are in the kitchen. She's washing the dishes, and he's drying. Gran is sitting in a chair by the fireplace, reading.

"Yeah, it's quiet," I say.

"Don't take this the wrong way, Hayley," Rupert says, "but you look awful."

"I feel pretty awful," I admit.

"Maybe you'd better lie down," Chloe suggests.

"I think that's a good idea." I head off to our room to be alone.

Even though I don't think that lying down is going to fix what's wrong with me.

Guts

By four o'clock, I feel like something is trying to claw its way out of my stomach. I drank a glass of ginger ale to settle my stomach, but it just seems to have made everything worse.

Chloe knocks on the door. "Hayley, are you okay?"

"No," I say weakly.

"Dad's here." Her voice is soft.

"Okay." I stand up and smooth my clothes. I splash a little water on my face, trying hard not to get it on my new dress. I take a deep breath. Then another. Then I fluff up the fake flower, which has wilted at my waist.

I head all the way downstairs and into the café to say good-bye to Mom and Gran. My dad is there, and I can tell that he and Mom have been arguing. They stop talking when they see me.

"How are you feeling?" Dad asks.

"Terrible," I tell him.

His blue eyes flash in irritation. "What's wrong?" he demands, as if I have gotten sick just to inconvenience him.

"My stomach." I shake my head. I feel awful, like I need to lie down again. I feel a trickle of sweat creep down the back of my neck.

"I don't think Hayley should go," Mom says.

Dad looks at her, then at me. "Is that what you want? To stay here?"

"I don't feel well."

"You don't have to eat anything," Dad says. "You can just sit there."

I put a hand on a tabletop to steady myself. Dad is dressed up. He's wearing a gray suit that looks new and a beautiful orange tie. He wants me to go to this dinner. I know the set of his jaw and the tone of his voice — I'm going.

"Okay," I say at last. "I'll just sit there."

"Hayley —" Mom says, but I just give her a hug.

"Bye, Mom. Bye, Gran."

"Good-bye, darling," Gran says. She has been listening to the entire conversation with a dark-eyed glower, and she shoots daggers at my father as he, Chloe, and I walk out the door.

Annie is waiting by the car. "Everyone ready?" she asks with a smile. "Oh, Hayley — is that — are those . . ." She's looking at my shoes, and her smile has disappeared.

"You can't wear high-tops to the country club," Dad announces. "Go change."

But my head is swimming, and my muscles ache. I think about the stairs to the apartment and feel dizzy. "I don't have any nice shoes." My voice sounds far away to me, like someone else is phoning it in.

"You don't have any heels?" Dad asks.

I'd thought that the dress actually looked kind of cool with high-tops. But I was telling the truth — the only nice pair of shoes I have that fit are sandals. And November in Massachusetts isn't sandal weather.

"Hayley needs to sit down," Chloe announces. "Can we please just go?"

"What about her shoes?" Dad asks.

"It's Thanksgiving, Dad," Chloe tells him. "Anybody who cares about her shoes is a jerk."

Way to go, Chloe, I think as Dad stands there awkwardly. Chloe never argues with anyone.

Anyway, she's right. I really, really do need to sit down.

Dad looks at his watch. "All right, let's get going. I don't want to be late." And we all pile into the Lexus.

In the backseat, Chloe takes my hand. I lean my head on her shoulder. "It's going to be okay," Chloe whispers.

I nod.

All I have to do is sit there, I think. *Just sit there.*

That's all.

Dad Was Right

I realize it before we even set foot in the restaurant. We pull up in front of an enormous white building with columns and bushes cut into the shape of swans. Yes, I'm serious. Swans. They're covered in white lights and glow softly in the foggy darkness.

I probably would have thought it was really pretty, if I didn't feel so horrible.

We pull up in a circular drive, and Dad gives the keys to a valet. Chloe helps me get out of the car, and I cling to her arm for support. And then we walk into this really elegant room with a marble floor and flower arrangements the size of my mom's car. I take one look at the enormous crystal chandelier and think, *Wrong shoes.*

Annie walks up to a man in a tuxedo. "Hello, Wilson," she says. "Are my parents here?"

"Good evening, Ms. Montri," Wilson says. "Yes, your parents are already seated. Will anyone else be joining you?" He nods at her, and she gestures to us.

Wilson looks us over. His eyes linger just a second on my high-tops, and one of his eyebrows lifts.

My dad huffs a sigh, and I can tell he wants to say something. Something along the lines of, "I *told* her not to wear those." But here is the thing — this place is actually too fancy for anyone to complain about your shoes.

"Right this way," Wilson says.

I spot Annie's parents right away — she looks just like her mother, who is elegantly dressed in a cream suit. Her father beams as we walk toward him, and his enormous smile makes me feel a bit better.

Annie introduces Dad to her parents, and I'm aware that my father is giving his heartiest handshake. Annie's dad smiles and shakes my hand, while her mother says a gentle hello and peers into my face with a slightly worried expression.

"Are you all right?" Mrs. Montri asks.

"Hayley isn't feeling well," Dad explains.

"Sit down, sit down!" Annie's father says.

We all take a seat. I place my napkin in my lap, but Chloe hesitates over hers. "Oh, I hate to unfold it," she says, looking at the swan.

"Isn't it lovely?" Mrs. Montri says. "They teach classes here on how to make them."

"Really?" Chloe asks, as if she's always been dying to learn to fold napkins.

"So, David, I hear you and Annie work together?" Mr. Montri asks, turning to my father.

"Yes, I'm an attorney."

"And what kind of car do you drive?" Mr. Montri asks.

"Dad!" Annie shakes her head and rolls her eyes.

My dad laughs and blushes slightly. "A Lexus," he admits. That car is his pride and joy.

Mr. Montri frowns slightly, and reaches for the bread basket. "Would anyone like to try some? They make the rolls here, and they're delicious."

"Dad owns a Cadillac dealership," Annie explains.

"Best car in the world," her father says fiercely. "Always buy American."

Annie sighs. "Oh, Dad."

My father squirms uncomfortably. "Um, Mrs. Montri — you're a doctor, I understand?"

"Yes," Mrs. Montri replies. "I've been in practice for over fifteen years."

"We came to this country almost twenty years ago with nothing," Mr. Montri says. "Nothing! And now — look at us!" He sends out his arm in a sweeping gesture, including the whole restaurant in his achievement.

"A real success story," my father says.

"People complain about this country." Mr. Montri leans toward my dad, as if he's challenging him to say a bad word about the USA. "But I tell you, there is no other place in the world with the opportunities America has."

Chloe passes me the bread basket. I can feel that the rolls are warm, and they smell wonderful, even though my guts are tossing. I wonder if a bite of bread might settle my stomach, like saltines are supposed to. I pick a roll out of the basket and put it down on my plate.

"Well, of course, China is growing rapidly," my father says.

"China!" Mr. Montri looks outraged. "China! China? There is no innovation in China. There is no leadership! China? The way they treat their workers — it's very bad!"

"Well, I —" My father looks to Annie for help, but she just shrugs.

"Dad loves to argue," Annie tells him.

My dad does not love to argue, and I see him squirming uncomfortably as Mr. Montri blusters on about the need for United States leadership in the world community. "This is what the Founding Fathers were dedicated to — ideals!

Equality of man! China? Their idea of equality is that everyone is treated the same — terribly!"

Finally, a silence falls over the table. I take a bite of my roll. And chew. And chew.

"Um, Hayley is learning a lot about the Founding Fathers in history class this year, right, Hayley?" Dad looks at me, as if he hopes that I'll be able to help him somehow.

And I want to. I really do. But I'm chewing.

Still chewing.

"Hayley?" Chloe asks. "Are you okay?"

I try to swallow. I can't.

I open my mouth to reply and throw up into the bread basket.

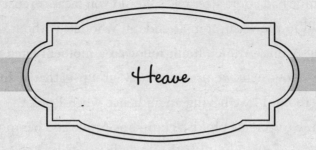

Heave

"Hayley? Hayley? Are you okay?" Annie is knocking on the door to the bathroom stall, where I'm kneeling over the toilet, heaving.

I don't answer her. I can't answer her. I'm sick.

The white marble floor is so cool under my knees. So clean. I never want to leave.

Besides, I can't come out — I can't go back into that restaurant. When I threw up, everyone stopped talking. Everyone stared at me. One eight-year-old boy in a navy blazer said, "Eeew!" and it echoed through the restaurant. I'd ruined their fancy Thanksgiving dinners that they'd paid a zillion dollars for.

But at least I was wearing my sneakers. I ran to the bathroom so fast that nobody at my table even had time to react.

Annie had come after me. "Would you please excuse us?" she said to the washroom attendant, who left without questioning Annie. Annie's mom followed a moment later, then Chloe. Now here we are — a cozy group gathered in the ladies' room. I love having an audience when I puke.

I heave up some pinkish chunks as Annie and her mother start to argue in Thai. I lie back on the marble, gasping, as the fight goes on.

"My mom wants to see you," Annie says at last.

I don't reply. I'm not coming out. Ever.

Mrs. Montri says something in a low voice, and a moment later, Chloe's face appears below the stall. "Hayley?"

"Sick," I mutter. Seriously, I can't say more.

My sister Spider-Mans under the door and crawls over to me. It's a lucky thing we're in a fancy restaurant. I wouldn't want my sister crawling all over the floor at a gas station.

"I thought you could use some company," Chloe says, taking my hand.

"I should've taken the handicapped stall," I manage to choke out. "Then everyone could come in."

Chloe laughs a little. "You look horrible."

"I know," I say from my place beside the toilet. "It's because of my shoes."

"Listen, Hayley, do you think you can come out?"

"No."

"You have to come out sometime."

"Maybe after they close."

Chloe brushes my hair away from my face. Some of it is stuck to the sides of my mouth. Only a sister would do that for you. "Hayley, I'm going to unlock the door, okay?"

"No."

"Mrs. Montri is a doctor. Besides . . ." She leans forward to whisper in my ear. "She might be our grandmother someday."

I sigh and wave my hand in an *I give up* gesture, so Chloe opens the door. Mrs. Montri walks in and kneels down beside me. "Thank you, Hayley, for letting me in," she says as she lifts my wrist. She stares at her watch for a few moments. Then she looks at my arm.

"It's all blotchy," Chloe says.

"Hives," Mrs. Montri tells her. "When they're this big, they're called plaques. Hayley, did you eat anything unusual earlier today? Get stung by a bee — something like that?"

"The paella?" Chloe suggests.

"Didn't it have lobster in it?" I ask. "I've never had that before."

Mrs. Montri nods. "Annie, help me get Hayley to her feet."

"I don't think I can sit through dinner," I say.

"We're leaving immediately," Mrs. Montri tells me. "We're just informing your father."

Annie and her mother work together, and in a moment, I'm standing. "Where are you taking me?"

"To my office," Mrs. Montri says.

Chloe dashes ahead, and I see my father react when she arrives at the table, pointing at us. The other diners in the restaurant are either oblivious or too polite to notice us — nobody looks up as I walk by. Except for the eight-year-old who said, "Eeew!" He watches me with a curled lip.

My dad stands up as I near the table. "Everything okay?" he asks.

"Yes," I say, just as Mrs. Montri says, "Hardly. Your daughter is having a severe allergic reaction. You see this?" She holds out my arm. "This is anaphylaxis. In severe cases, the throat closes. We're leaving to get some medication."

I want to say something to comfort my dad, but Mrs. Montri is already steering me through the restaurant, with Annie and Chloe trailing behind.

Confession: What I Wanted to Tell My Dad

I TOLD YOU I WAS SICK! I told you! I told you! You don't LISTEN! You have to have what YOU want! Nobody else matters!

I hope that Annie's parents think you're a jerk.

Confession about That Confession: I Never Would Have Said Any of That

It's all true, though.

It's just that there are some things you can't say.

Embarrassed

"Sweetie?" Mom steps hesitantly into the dark living room. "Your dad is on the phone."

"I'm too sick to talk to him."

Mom hovers a moment. She glances at Meghan, who is seated on the couch beside me. Blue light plays across Meghan's face, the glow from the movie we're watching. Meghan shrugs a little, and my mother sighs.

"Okay, Hayley," Mom says at last. "I'll tell him."

We watch a little more of *A Christmas Story*. Meghan called this morning to see how Thanksgiving had gone. I told her about the whole scene the night before, and she showed up this afternoon with flowers and the movie, which is one of my all-time favorites. I watch it every year.

"Kind of mad at your dad, huh?" Meghan says.

"Yep." I keep my eyes on the screen.

"Do you want to talk about it?"

"Nope."

Meghan picks up the remote and hits PAUSE. "I kind of think you should talk about it," she says.

"Stop being bossy," I tell her.

"I try, but I can't help it!" She leans her head against the arm of the chair. "You have no idea how hard it is." Meghan gives me a big, weepy-eyed look. "You should feel sorry for me!"

"Look, I told my dad I was sick, but he didn't care. He only cared about my shoes, and the fact that I was embarrassing him. Well, good — I hope I did embarrass him when I barfed into the bread basket."

"Happy Thanksgiving," Meghan says.

"Right." I put my face in my hands and take a few deep breaths while Meghan pats me awkwardly on the shoulder. "So — don't you have any instructions? Or, like, words of wisdom?"

Meghan shakes her head.

"Not even an inspirational quote?"

"Hang in there?"

"That doesn't even make sense."

"Okay, then, no. I don't have anything inspiring to say. I just thought that talking might make you feel better."

"It didn't."

"Well, I told you — not all of my ideas are winners."

That, at least, makes me laugh.

"Speaking of — Ben Habib called me. Seems he's figured out that I'm his secret admirer."

I gasp. "I can't believe you've been here for an hour and you're only mentioning this now! What did he say?"

"He was really sweet." Meghan picks up a throw pillow and hugs it to her chest. "I mean, he didn't quote Shakespeare or say I was the girl of his dreams or anything, but — he sounded kind of . . . *regretful*. Or maybe that was all in my mind. Anyway, it was nice to think that maybe he wished things could've turned out differently. But he said that his parents don't approve of dating before you're really ready to get married."

"What did you say?"

"I told him we should just get married."

"Meg!" I squeal. "You're so crazy!"

"No, I didn't really say that." Meghan grins at me, showing her dimples. "That really would've been insane. What I said was, 'That's a bummer.' He said, 'Well, I guess I'll just keep this note in the same place I've got the ones from all the other girls,' and then we both laughed and we said good-bye."

"Wow," I said. "Wow."

"Yeah." Meghan tugs at a tassel on the pillow. "I knew it would end this way."

"So, why did you do all that stuff? The whole secret-admirer campaign?"

"I just wanted Ben to know how I felt."

"But — aren't you embarrassed?" I couldn't imagine being Meghan and having to go to school and see Ben on Monday.

"Why would I be?" Meghan asks, and I realize something — she's serious. She does not understand why someone would hide feelings. She doesn't care if the whole grade thinks she's a fool.

"I think you're amazing, Meg," I say.

"Really?" Her face brightens. "You really think I'm amazing? I think you're amazing, too."

I laugh. "Okay."

"No, I'm serious! I wouldn't say it if I didn't mean it." She reaches out and touches my arm.

I smile. "I know you wouldn't, Meg."

Olive-Oil Cupcakes
(makes approximately 12 cupcakes)

Okay, I know this may not sound delicious. But you should trust me on this one. Sometimes it's good to take a risk.

INGREDIENTS:
- 1 cup milk
- 1 teaspoon apple cider vinegar
- 1-1/4 cups all-purpose flour
- 3/4 teaspoon baking powder
- 1/2 teaspoon baking soda
- 1/2 teaspoon salt
- 3/4 cup granulated sugar
- 1/3 cup olive oil (Try to find a fruity olive oil, such as one made from Spanish Arbequina olives, so that the flavor is more pronounced.)

INSTRUCTIONS:
1. Preheat the oven to 350°F. Line a muffin pan with cupcake liners.
2. Whisk the milk and apple cider vinegar in a

measuring cup and set aside for a few minutes to curdle.

3. Sift together the flour, baking powder, baking soda, and salt into a bowl, and mix.

4. In a separate large bowl, mix the curdled milk with the sugar, and olive oil. Add the dry ingredients to the wet ones a little bit at a time, and combine using a whisk or a handheld mixer, stopping to scrape down the sides of the bowl a few times, until smooth and no lumps remain.

5. Fill cupcake liners two-thirds of the way full and bake for 22–24 minutes. Transfer to a cooling rack, and let cool completely before frosting.

Rosemary Frosting

INGREDIENTS:

    2 sprigs fresh rosemary

    1/4 cup milk

    1 cup margarine or butter

    1 teaspoon vanilla extract

    3-1/2 cups confectioners' sugar

1. Remove the rosemary leaves from the branches and chop them roughly. In a small saucepan, gently heat the milk until warm. When very small bubbles appear on the edges, remove the pan from heat. Add the rosemary leaves and set aside for 10 minutes to steep.

2. In a large bowl, cream the margarine or butter until lighter in color, then add the vanilla extract.

3. Strain the rosemary leaves from the milk. Measure the remaining milk to ensure that you still have 1/4 cup of milk, and add more fresh milk if necessary. Reserve some of the rosemary

leaves and chop them finely to make about 1 tablespoon.

4. Slowly add the confectioners' sugar in 1/2-cup batches and mix until fully incorporated, adding the milk in small amounts in between batches. Add the finely chopped rosemary leaves and beat on high speed until the frosting is light and fluffy, about 3–7 minutes.

From the Phone Files: Part 2

"Hayley?"

"Hi, Dad."

"How are you feeling?"

"Okay."

"Still itching?"

"The hives come back every couple hours. Then I just take another Benadryl. They're supposed to stop after a few days."

"That's good."

"Yeah."

"Look, Hayley, I didn't realize you were so sick. I just thought that — maybe — you didn't want to come."

"Yeah."

"So — is that all you have to say? 'Yeah'?"

"Look, Dad. It's okay. I'm not sick anymore. There's no point in feeling bad about it, okay?"

"Yeah. Okay. But, Hayley, I just wanted —"

"Dad? Mom is calling me. Can I talk to you later?"

"Sure, Hayley. We can talk later."

"Bye."

"Bye."

Confession:
I Wish I Were Like Meghan

I'm not saying that Meghan is perfect. She isn't. As we know, she's a bit bossy and kinda crazy.

But.

But at least she isn't afraid of stuff. She tells people how she feels. She's honest.

How many people can really say that they're honest?

I'm not. I just told my dad that I had to go because my mom was calling me.

Lie.

I can't even tell my own father how I'm really feeling.

Meghan would've told him.

Maybe I should ask *her* to tell him.

Dumped

"Jeez, they're loading the muskets again," Meghan says as she covers her ears. A moment later, there's a loud *crack*, like a cannon blast. "Why do they let those guys march in every single parade? My eardrums had barely recovered from Veterans Day."

The Revolutionary War re-enactors keep marching in step to the fife and drum. I have to wonder how many real minutemen were overweight and wore glasses. About 90 percent of them, according to this sampling.

"I love those revolutionaries," I say. "They're dedicated."

"Oh, look! There's the Big Babies Portable Band." Meghan points to a loony group of people in red and orange. They're half-marching, half-dancing as they play an upbeat tune.

"Those guys are awesome." The Big Babies sometimes just show up downtown, especially if there's some kind of protest going on.

A dreary clown tosses some candy from the back of a vintage truck, and a group of young kids runs to grab it. Our town's Thanksgiving Parade is tiny. It always happens the Saturday after Thanksgiving and only lasts about ten minutes. The good thing is that it makes a double loop around the block. "The parade so nice that it goes around twice," my dad calls it.

Still, it's really cute, and it's close to my old house, so we used to come every year. It's funny — sometimes it seems like half the town is in the parade, and the other half is lining the streets. And sometimes it seems like *most* of the town is in the parade, and the leftovers are lining the streets.

Today, the streets are pretty packed. I scan the crowd across the way. Groups of children are holding balloons from the local bank. Moms are sipping coffee; dads have kids on their shoulders. And there — right across from us — is Artie. She's standing with Chang and Kelley, her new best friends.

"Where's Devon?" I say, half to myself. "I didn't realize Artie would let him out of her sight." That's mean, and I know it. I feel like a jerk even as the words leave my lips. But it's too late — Meghan has heard me.

"Didn't you know?" she asks. "Devon told Artie that he wasn't into her."

"What?" My heart drops to my feet and flops onto the pavement. Now I feel totally awful. And yet . . .

There's another part of me that's actually happy.

Happy!

Because if Devon isn't into Artie, could it mean that he's into . . . somebody else?

Like, maybe somebody I know?

Like, somebody I know *well*?

Like, in case you're not getting this — *me*?

All of these thoughts are racing through my mind, and Meghan is just standing there, watching a bunch of Shriners do figure eights in their teeny-tiny cars. And I want to tell her that my whole life might conceivably change because of this news, and I'm about to open my mouth when I hear someone say, "Where's Santa?" and when I look over, I see Kyle standing not five feet from us.

"We want Santa!" he shouts.

"Hey, Kyle. It's Hayley and Meghan."

"Oh, hey! Santa hasn't come by yet, has he?"

"They usually save him for the end," Meghan says.

"As if I have any idea when that is," Kyle tells her.

"Here comes the Community Band." A flatbed truck drives slowly by, carrying a group of my former neighbors. They're playing "Jingle Bells."

"They're pretty good," Kyle says, and I nod. "But where's all the candy? People usually give me candy at this parade. Not to complain."

At that moment, a man in a suit walks over to Kyle, hands him a candy cane, then walks on.

"Perfect timing!" Kyle shouts after him. "Who was that, anyway?" he asks me.

"The mayor."

Kyle laughs, then stops. "Wait — seriously?"

"Yeah, the new one," Meghan agrees. "Who just got elected a couple of weeks ago."

"Awesome!" Kyle unwraps the candy cane and takes a lick. "Glad my parents voted for him."

"I'm glad my parents voted for him because of his stance on local issues," Meghan says, almost huffily.

Kyle grins. "Meghan, you're a trip," he says, which makes her laugh.

"Here comes Santa," I say.

"Where?" Meghan stands on her tiptoes.

"He's in the fire truck," I tell her. "You can barely see

him. That wasn't the smartest move." The sight of the fire truck sends a worm of anxiety through my stomach, and I find myself scanning the crowd. I'm still not feeling 100-percent well after VomitFest, and it doesn't take much to make me queasy. A light sweat breaks out on my forehead. But I don't see the face I'm looking for. I gnaw my thumbnail, which has only started to grow out.

"I can't see him at all!" Meghan complains.

"Well, then — we're even!" Kyle says.

"But you were the one who was so desperate to see Santa," Meghan points out.

"I'm not desperate to *see* him," Kyle corrects her. "I'm just desperate for him to get here, so that they'll start handing out the free cookies and cider."

This is another annual tradition — the parade ends at the Civic Center, where there's a Santa meet and greet that involves tons of sweets and screaming kids. The whole idea of walking over there makes my nausea return. "So — are we going?" Kyle asks.

"Sure," Meghan says. "Let's head over there before they circle around again. Then we'll be first in line."

"Brilliant," Kyle agrees. "You coming, Hayley?"

"You guys go on without me," I say. "I've got to head home."

"Are you sure?" Meghan asks.

I nod, though this isn't — strictly speaking — true. It's just that I've had a thought. An idea, really.

Kyle is sweet. And funny. And really smart.

And Meghan is cool. And funny. And really smart.

I know that, even though she isn't showing it, Meghan is probably still disappointed over the whole Ben scene. But . . . maybe she might like Kyle, if she got to know him.

"I'll see you guys on Monday, okay?" I say.

"Bye, Hayley!" Meghan calls cheerfully, and in a moment, she and Kyle have disappeared into the swirling eddies of people trailing the end of the parade.

I sigh and start to walk to the corner. Then I take a sudden left.

I'm not going home. Not yet.

There's someone I missed at the parade, and I'm going to go find out where she is.

Sarah

It's hard to tell if anyone's home just by looking at the quiet house. The leaves have been raked, but the grass is beginning to fade to a patchwork of brown and green. The blooms on the mums are starting to shrivel, but the fire bushes line the driveway with brilliant red.

This is Marco's yard. It's right next to my old yard, which is a disaster zone of plastic toys and dead leaves.

I pause, looking up at the front door, which is as white as a blank piece of paper. I won't knock on it. I've *never* knocked on it. We always used the back door.

I walk up the driveway and past the back deck. I'm about to turn toward the rear entrance when I catch a movement out of the corner of my eye — the curtain in the tree house fluttered. *He's up there*, I think, and for a moment, I'm back in third grade, when Marco and I would spend afternoons eating Oreos and reading *Mad* magazine in our tree house. And it really was *our* tree house, in some ways, even though it was in Marco's backyard. Our fathers built it together the summer before second grade, over Marco's mother's objections. She was worried about safety — what if we fell out? — but there was no talking our fathers out of it. "A kid should have a tree house," Marco's dad said, and my father agreed.

I'm climbing the ladder before I even have time to think.

When I poke my head through the floor, Marco is sitting there with wide eyes, as if he expected a monster or a murderer to appear. "Hi," I say.

"Oh. Hi." A little color returns to his cheeks, but not much.

"What's up?" I haul myself onto the platform and sit down across from him.

Marco watches me, almost wary, as if I might spring. "Just thinking."

"I was looking for you guys at the parade," I say.

"We weren't there."

"Sarah's not into fire trucks anymore?" Marco's sister has always been obsessed with emergency-response vehicles. She knows all about fire trucks, and could probably even drive one, if someone would let her.

"Didn't you know? She's at a residential school now." Marco stands up and pulls back the curtain to look out the window. This tree house used to seem huge, but now there's barely room to move around.

"Boarding school?" I ask. "Does she like it?"

Marco's shoulder lifts, then dips. "It's hard to tell."

"Maybe a special school is a good idea — she can get the help she needs."

Marco looks pained. "That's what *they* said."

We sit in silence for a moment. I want to talk to Marco about the test — the fact that we cheated, and how it made me feel. But I can't force the words out. He looks at me, his eyebrows slightly lifted, and I get the sense that there's something that he wants to say, too. But neither one of us speaks. We just let the silence stretch between us.

I know I should just tell him what I'm thinking, but I can tell he's sad already. I don't want to make it worse. So I stay silent. And then the moment is broken by a voice calling Marco's name. It's his mother.

"I'll see you," Marco says.

And he leaves me sitting in his tree house, which used to be our tree house, all by myself.

Confession: I'm Glad Sarah Is Gone

$\mathcal{L}$ook, Sarah was difficult. It was embarrassing to go out in public with her. I know I'm not supposed to say that, but it's true. She was in her own world most of the time, and loud noises could sometimes make her scream. She would hit herself. People would stare. First at her, then at us. Then at her again.

Marco has always loved Sarah. She drives him nuts, too, sometimes, of course. But they have their own equation — she's calmer around him. He's the little brother, but he likes to protect her. I've seen him take on much older boys who were teasing her. I know it must be hard for him without her here.

Still, I think it's better that she's gone.

I've said before that Marco never really liked to have friends over at his house. Well, one of the few times I was there, I noticed that there was a lock on the outside of Sarah's bedroom door. I realized then that Marco's parents must be locking her in there sometimes.

It sent a shiver through me.

I don't know — maybe lots of parents do that. But mine never would have. It struck me as wrong, and maybe even dangerous. Marco's parents were strict — the lock on the door made me wonder about other ways they might "discipline" Sarah.

I never told anyone about that. I never even mentioned it to Marco. It felt too scary.

Anyway, that's why I'm glad that Sarah went away.

Glad for Sarah, I mean.

WWMMD?

Don't chicken out, I tell myself as I scan the nearly empty hallway. The first bell hasn't rung yet, but people are milling around, heading to lockers. *Just pretend you're Meghan.* What Would Meghan Markerson Do? Meghan would tell Devon how she felt; that's what she'd do. She wouldn't beat around the bush, either. She'd hire a skywriter or set off fireworks or something.

I look down at the cake pop in my hand. It's covered in white chocolate, and has a single red candy heart stuck to the top. I finally got the chocolate to go on evenly, and this looks like it could be on the cover of *Cake Pop Monthly* magazine. It's the Hayley equivalent of fireworks.

I like to think I learned something from the moment I let pass by with Marco. I should have said something about the test then, when we were alone in the tree house. Now I'll never get that moment back, and we'll probably never talk about it. Maybe we won't need to. Maybe Marco felt as bad as I did. But I don't know.

I check my watch, then dig my assignment notebook out of my purse and pretend to scan it for some kind of Very Important Information. Really, I'm just waiting for Devon to head toward his homeroom, hoping to catch him before the first bell rings. I look over my shoulder and say a tiny prayer of thanks that Artie is nowhere in sight.

"Hey, Hayley!" Devon gives me that warm smile, the one that melts my kneecaps and makes me feel like I'm going to ooze all over the floor. "Is that for me?"

He knows! My face is practically consumed in flames, but I force myself to hand him the cake pop. Suddenly, the red heart seems incredibly obvious, worse than skywriting. "Um, yeah."

"Seriously?" Devon smiles. "I was kidding!"

"Oh — you were? I — I just wanted to preview the cake pops, you know, before I put them out at the fund-raiser. . . ." *Not true. Stop talking. You're messing everything up!*

Devon takes a bite out of the cake pop. "Oh, man — I'm going into sugar shock! This thing is awesome!"

My heart flops like an awkward toad. "You like it?"

"You're some kind of crazy cupcake genius, Hayley. I really owe you for doing this fund-raiser. Honestly, I kind of can't wait until this whole play is over. I'll finally have some free time."

"Well, uh — hey — do . . ." It's really hard to think when all of the blood in your body is rushing to your head. "Uh . . . do you want to go to —" *Can hardly breathe!* "A movie, uh, next weekend? Or something? Since you'll have time . . ." I try to gulp in some air.

"Oh, sure," Devon says as he takes another bite of the cake pop. "That might be . . ."

I'm hanging there, waiting for the end of that sentence. Fun? Boring? Weird? Awkward? But just as I'm about to say, "What would it be, Devon?" a pretty girl with dark hair and large brown eyes steps out of a classroom and grabs on to Devon's arm with a possessive smile.

It's Trina Bachman, and she's hanging on Devon like a Christmas ornament.

"Hey, Trina, taste this," Devon says, holding the cake pop to her lips.

"Mmmm," she says as she nibbles a bite. Then she touches her lips as if she's afraid her lip gloss might have been mussed by a crumb. "So sweet."

Devon cocks his head and smiles at me. "So — we'll chat later?" he asks.

My throat has swelled so much that I can hardly force air through it. But I do. I manage to whisper, "Sure," as Devon walks off with Trina. Now I know why he broke up with Artie. It was because of another girl — but that girl wasn't me.

Why did I think this was a good idea? I wonder as hot tears threaten to choke me. *I'm not Meghan Markerson.*

There's a reason I thought she was crazy. Maybe she can confess her feelings without getting her heart crushed . . . but I guess I can't.

Guilty

See me after class.

I'm staring at the note as the seconds click by on the clock above Mr. Carter's desk.

See me after class.

We've been back from our holiday for three days, but Mr. Carter has just handed back everyone's tests. Everyone's but mine. And Marco's. He gave us each a note.

Meghan noticed, of course. She frowned when she saw that. *What's up?* she mouthed, but I just shook my head and looked over at Marco. He was staring at his desk, cheeks burning.

I can't stop those last ten seconds from slipping away. The bell rings, and I gather my things and head to the front. Marco trails behind me, looking at the floor, the whiteboard, watching the other students file out — his eyes are every-where but on mine.

Mr. Carter is glaring at Marco as we step up to his desk. Our teacher rolls his chair backward a bit and folds his arms across his chest. He waits until the last student has filed out and says, "I know that one of you copied off of the other dur-ing the last test." His eyes flicker to my face, almost with a look of pity, then settle back on Marco.

"How do you know?" Marco asks.

Mr. Carter opens a folder and pulls out the tests. He points to a problem he has circled on the second page. I see it immediately — I made a careless error while simplifying one of the fractions in the problem. "Fourteen divided by two does not equal six. It's possible for one person to make a sloppy mistake like that, but not for two students to make the same sloppy mistake. A *second grader* knows what four-teen divided by two is." He hisses on the word *second grader* and sneers at Marco, and I just wish I could punch him in the face.

"I think that one of you copied from the other, but I can't prove who did the copying," Mr. Carter says. "So. The grade on these exams — minus this mistake — is a ninety-six. Since one of you did the work, and one didn't, I'll be generous" — he grins the ugliest grin I've ever seen — "I'll let you split the grade." Then he narrows his eyes and looks at Marco. "In case you can't do the math, that's a forty-eight for each of you." He sits back in his chair, smug. "Unless one of you wants to confess. Then each of you can have the grade you really earned — a zero and a ninety-six." Mr. Carter stares hard at Marco, as if he hopes to bore a hole through him with his gaze. Marco has turned pale, and looks like he's about to throw up.

Mr. Carter wants him to squirm, I realize, and before I know what I'm doing, I hear myself say, "It was me."

Mr. Carter's eyebrows go up. "What?"

"It was me," I repeat, "I did it. I cheated."

The room is silent for a long moment. Mr. Carter clearly did not expect this outcome. "I —" he says after a moment. "I —" But he can't seem to finish the thought.

"I'm sorry, it won't happen again." I feel tears burning at the back of my throat, and I can't take anymore, so I turn and run out.

"Hayley!" Marco shouts. I hear his footsteps behind me, and feel him grab my arm. The hallway is still crowded with students going to classes, and a few people stare as I try to shake off my friend. "Let go."

Marco places his hands on my shoulders. "Hayley, what did you just do?"

"Just say thank you," I tell him. "Okay? You know you can never pull your grade up from a zero. I can."

Marco shakes his head.

"You were never going to tell him, anyway," I whisper.

"I would have," Marco insists. "I was about to."

I look him dead in the eye. "Then why didn't you?"

The question hangs there between us for a moment, dark and ugly. Here it is — my Meghan Moment. I've finally said it.

"I don't care," I say at last, because I can't think of anything else. Marco's hands fall away from my shoulders.

I walk away from him, and he lets me.

"Are you okay?"

I feel a gentle tug at my elbow, and when I turn, I see Meghan standing there, watching me with a worried expression. "What's wrong?"

The tears do strangle me then, and I have to struggle to force words out. "Everything" is all I manage to say. "Marco and Devon and my dad and even Artie — just . . . everything."

"Yeah, I heard about Devon and Trina. Sorry."

"You said you thought he liked *me*!"

She winces. "It's kind of hard to tell with Devon. Don't you think? I mean, I think maybe he's kind of flirty with everyone. I think even the lunch ladies have a crush on him."

I sigh.

"Come on," Meghan says, pulling my arm. "I want to show you something."

I'm like a limp rag — too boneless to resist — as she herds me to the stairwell. "Where are we going?" I ask as I follow her up two flights of stairs.

"One more," Meghan says.

"To the roof?"

"Yep." She touches the red bar on the door that reads FIRE ALARM WILL SOUND.

"Wait!"

Meghan ignores me, and the door is silent as it swings open.

"You've done this before."

"Yep," Meghan agrees as she leads me out onto the black roof. Beyond us is a blue sky. A stiff breeze blows by, making me shiver. Meghan walks to the small overhang at the edge of the roof. She sits down on it.

"You're making me nervous," I tell her.

Meghan laughs. "As usual." She waves at me. "Come here."

"Are you going to push me over?"

"Don't tempt me."

I walk over. When I look down, I can see the center courtyard dotted with clumps and clusters of students. I can see Artie and her new friends on the steps almost directly below us. I see Marco's soccer friends. After a moment, he joins them. I'm high above them all; it's easy to imagine that they're dolls, or pieces of a jigsaw puzzle that I need to put together.

Meghan follows my gaze, and her eyes land on Marco. "You told me once that I don't know what Marco's life is like. You're right. But I know that it's probably really complicated. And I know that he cares about you and doesn't want to make you miserable."

I shiver a little and hunch inside my sweater. I'm not dressed to be outdoors. It's lunch period — everyone else has grabbed their jackets.

Meghan's gaze shifts to my face. "Still, he's got his life, and you've got yours. You can't fix everything for him."

"No." My voice is a whisper, and it nearly disappears on the wind.

"Everyone looks so small from up here." Meghan looks up at the white clouds on the blue sky. "And I guess we look small from up there."

"You mean, like, from God's point of view?"

"I'm talking about perspective, Hayley."

"What's that supposed to mean?"

Meghan purses her lips and folds her arms across her chest. " 'Everything we see is a perspective, not the truth.' "

I think about that for a moment. "Bumper sticker?" I ask.

"Of course — I have zero deep thoughts of my own. But I'm thinking about Artie, too. I have no idea what her life is like, either, or why she's acting like a stone cold . . ." Meghan shrugs. "I don't know — stone. And I have zero clue what's up with your dad, except that his brain isn't really where it's supposed to be right now, you know? But I do know that it sounds like your dad has a lot going on in his life and Artie is totally jealous of you. And I think they'll probably both get over it."

I remember the day Artie confessed to me that she had a crush on Marco. But Marco was never as close to Artie as he was to me. He even kissed me once, but that's a whole other story. At first, I didn't believe that Artie was jealous of me. But in my heart, I know that Meghan is right. You don't just turn on a friend that way for no reason at all.

Maybe all of that stuff with Devon was just her way of trying to get even.

Now I really feel sorry for her. For both of us. Our friendship is over — and for what? "What if they don't get over it?" I ask.

"Life goes on," Meghan says. "This stuff will all pass, one way or the other. I swear, Hayley, in ten years, you probably won't even remember how miserable you were, or anything else about this day."

The bell rings, and I watch the little people below me start to trickle toward the front double doors. In a few moments, I'll have to walk back down the stairs, rejoin them. But, right now, I feel light, like I'm closer to the sky than the ground. I look over at my friend, who is watching me with a sweet smile on her face. Her blue eyes are laughing, and — suddenly — I realize that I'm happy to be up here with her, free from the drama below. "You're wrong, Meg — I *will* remember this day," I tell her, and I mean it.

Grounded Again

"Hayley?" Mom's dark eyes are on me the minute I walk into the café. "I got a call from one of your teachers — Mr. Carter?" She comes out from behind the counter. "Let's sit down."

She leads me across the Tea Room to the table by the window. We sit down, and Mom gazes at me, like I'm a puzzle she can't quite solve.

I feel myself shriveling under her gaze. "What did he say?" I manage to squeak out.

"That you cheated. In math?" Mom shakes her head. "I told him that he must have made a mistake, but he said that you admitted it?"

"Yeah."

"What happened?"

"What he said — I cheated."

Mom nods, her eyes never leaving my face. I can't hold her gaze, though. I look down at the table and run my fingertip over a chip in the wood. "Do you want to tell me more about it?" she presses.

"Not really."

"That wasn't really a question, Hayley. What happened?"

I took a deep breath. "I let Marco copy my test."

"So you're both getting zeroes?"

"No — I told Mr. Carter that I copied off of Marco, so I get the zero."

"Hayley — why?"

"Because Mr. Carter hates Marco. He wants to see him fail."

"But Marco cheated —"

"I cheated, too. I let him copy my answers."

Mom turns her face toward the window and looks out. Finally, she turns back to me. "Look, Hayley, I'm grounding you again. You're already in trouble at school, so I'll give you a break at home — one week."

I nod. It's more than fair, really.

"I know that Marco is your good friend," Mom goes on. "But this doesn't make sense. You have to protect yourself a little."

"I know."

"You can't just do what Marco wants."

"I know."

"Now this is going to affect your grade."

"I know." I'm thinking that if I keep agreeing with her, maybe she'll stop talking.

"Hayley, I thought you learned this lesson in third grade —"

And that's when I shove back my chair. "Look, Mom — you're right. I know you're right. But I —" I shake my head, because I don't know how to explain what I'm feeling, or why I did what I did. I just did it. That's all.

As I walk toward the stairs at the back of the café, the sweet smell of cinnamon washes over me like a deep, warm wave. How can something smell so wonderful when I feel like pieces of my body are about to fall off and scatter across the wooden floor?

Confession: Third Grade

Mom is right. I should've learned my lesson in third grade. Marco got me into trouble then, too.

Sarah has always had a thing for fire trucks. I have memories — early memories — of her pointing out fire trucks, explaining their different parts and how they work, talking about how firefighters locate a fire. Fire hoses can spew water at a pressure of almost three hundred pounds per square inch — did you know that? Sarah knew it.

Whenever she got nervous, or bored, or whatever, she liked to go find a fire truck. She would even sometimes leave the special classroom she was in to go looking for them. They don't seem too relaxing to me, but Sarah always calmed down once she was at the fire station.

One day, when we were in third grade, Marco went looking for Sarah during recess. He couldn't find her anywhere.

There was a substitute teacher that morning, and Sarah was usually freaked out by new people. When Marco asked the sub where Sarah was, the teacher said she had gone to the bathroom. Well, Marco knew that wasn't true, because Sarah was terrified of the sound of the toilet flushing. There was no way she would go by herself.

Artie and I found Marco sitting under a tree, digging in the dirt with a stick. When he saw us, he stood up. "Come on," he said.

"Where are we going?" I asked.

"To the firehouse."

"Won't we get in trouble?" Artie wanted to know.

Marco scowled at the teachers, who were huddled in a corner of the asphalt, chatting. "They won't even notice we're gone, believe me."

In the end, Artie didn't go, but I did.

It was only five blocks to the firehouse, and we ran the whole way. We were half a block away when we saw Sarah. She was standing near the open garage door, talking to herself. I knew that she was reciting everything she knew about the truck.

We had almost reached her when a police car pulled up, looking for Sarah and us. The officer took us to the police station and called our parents. Marco and I were terrified, but Sarah really seemed to enjoy the ride. I guess a patrol car is almost as exciting as a fire truck.

I found out later that our teacher had noticed when Marco and I failed to show up in the classroom after recess. And that Artie was the one who told her where we went.

Remember that fight Artie and I had in third grade? When she didn't talk to me for a week? This was that fight.

I mean, I understood why Artie told on us. What we did was wrong. But Artie never understood why we had gone after Sarah in the first place. Artie never understood how much Marco loved his sister, or that he would have done anything to make sure she was safe.

But I understood it.

I guess people do the wrong thing for the right reasons sometimes. Or maybe that's just what we tell ourselves.

After the Musical

Soft yellow light pours like butter across the concrete in front of the café. I'm tired, but glad to be back at the Tea Room. I made fifty cake pops for the musical and only have three left. I did what I said I would, and now I can forget about Artie and Devon for a while.

It's Friday night, and the café is busy as I walk in through the front door, holding the almost-empty box. Gran looks up from the register and smiles. Someone in a dark coat is sitting on a stool at the counter. He turns, and I see that it's Marco.

I hesitate, suddenly unable to move forward.

"Need help?" Marco asks. He walks over to me and reaches for the box.

"I've got it," I tell him, and I grab it away. But Marco is

already holding it. We get into a silly little tug-of-war over the box.

"Please," Marco says finally. "Let me." I look into his large, dark eyes, then look down at the floor.

"All right." I give him the box, unsure whether I've just given in or whether it's okay to let him help.

He stands there, arms wrapped around the cardboard. "Um, where do you want this?"

"You can just put it in the back, in Mom's office. But take the cake pops out."

Marco nods and disappears in the back as I shrug off my jacket and step up to the counter. It's a little strange to be on the customers' side.

"Did you enjoy the play?" Gran asks as she sets a plate before me. She has placed two of her famous petit fours at the center.

"Not really."

"Ah," Gran says. She nods like she understands perfectly, which she probably does. She smiles as Marco returns, and then she bustles off to help a customer.

Marco flops onto the stool beside mine. There is a scone on the plate in front of him, but he's still wearing his coat, which makes it seem like he's about to jump up and run out the door at any moment. "I did it," he says.

"Thanks," I tell him.

"No, I mean — I told Mr. Carter what happened. That I cheated, that it wasn't you." He stares into my eyes. "I told him after school today."

I look down at my plate, unsure what to make of this. Instead, I study my petit fours. One of the tiny cakes is decorated with a red flower. The other is chocolate with a zigzag of vanilla. They're beautiful and perfect.

Marco seems to need to fill up the silence. "I told him that I was really desperate to get a decent grade on the test because I didn't want to get kicked off the soccer team, and I told him that you'd been trying to help me understand fractions, but then I just copied off of you. . . ." His voice trails off. "I told him all that. And I can tell your mom, too, if you want."

"I already explained the whole thing," I say. I push my plate away. Suddenly, I can't bear to chew up those perfect petit fours. I stand up and fold my coat over my arm. "I'm a little tired," I say, and start to walk away.

"Hayley?" Marco calls.

For a moment, I consider pretending that I haven't heard him. I really don't have the energy to talk more right now. But he calls again, "Hayley?" and I don't want him to come after me. I turn to face him.

"There's this art exhibit downtown. Sculptures of giant Twinkies. Do you — do you want to go? Together, I mean."

I'm not sure, but in the end, I say, "Okay," because — really — I guess I never can say no to Marco.

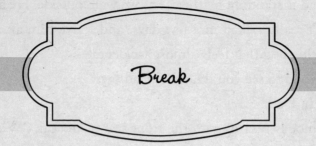

Break

"You're coming, aren't you?" Chloe hovers in the doorway to our bedroom, shifting her weight from one foot to the other.

"Why are you asking?" I ask as I peer out the window. I'm seated at my desk, and I look down at the Lexus that has just pulled up in front of the café. Dad is double-parked. He has the hazards on, even though there's an open parking space half a block away. Maybe he can't see it, though. I can see everything from my window.

"It won't be fun without you." Chloe shoves her fists into her coat pockets.

I imagine poor Chloe, sitting in the car with Dad and Annie, trying to act cheerful and pretend that nothing is wrong. She really thinks that it's her job to make everyone happy. "I'm coming," I tell her.

Dad is standing by the car as we walk outside. He and I haven't really talked in a few days, and I give him an awkward side-hug that feels almost accidental.

"Good to see you, Hayley," Dad says.

"Hi, Dad."

Chloe is peering into the front seat of the car. "Where's Annie?"

Dad is wearing aviator-style sunglasses, so I can't really read the expression in his eyes when he says, "I thought it would be just us today."

Chloe's face scrunches up. "Why?"

"Because I wanted some time with my girls."

We climb into the car. I sit in the front beside Dad, Chloe sits in the back. Dad grips the steering wheel and pulls into traffic. We pull up to a stoplight, and I realize that I have no idea where we're going. "What's the plan?"

"I thought we'd just head over to my apartment. Maybe watch a DVD or something," Dad says. "Cook dinner together."

That thought hangs in the car for a moment, like a wonderful scent. Just us and Dad, watching a movie. "That sounds good," I say, but it really sounds more than good to me — it sounds perfect.

Dad looks at me so long that the car behind us honks. Neither of us realized that the light had turned green. Dad puts his foot on the gas and pulls through the intersection. "Listen, Hayley," he says at last, keeping his eyes on the road. "There are a lot of things I would do differently, if I could. I'm . . . trying."

Silence fills the car, and I wonder if my dad has just apologized to me. I think so. He reaches out his hand, and I interlace my fingers in his. He keeps the other hand on the steering wheel. We drive like that for a while.

"What are we making for dinner?" asks a small voice from the backseat.

"I don't know," Dad admits. "I don't really have anything in the house. Let's go to the food co-op. What would you girls like?"

"Can we have steak?" Chloe asks, suddenly brightening.

"And baked potatoes," I put in.

"Sure. We'll make a salad, too. What should we have for dessert?" Dad grins as he asks this.

"Cupcakes!" Chloe shouts from the backseat.

"I guess I'm in charge of that," I say.

Dad pulls his fingers away from mine as he changes lanes. He flips on the radio. It's the local station — the one he and I used to listen to all the time at home. They play a random mix of music, from folk to funk. Right now it's an alternative song that I've heard a couple of times.

"Change the station, please," Chloe announces. She prefers pop music.

Dad turns it up and whistles along with the song. I start to whistle, too.

"Come on, you guys, can't we listen to the other station?" Chloe claps her hands over her ears, but she's giggling.

Dad smiles at me and I laugh. I turn the music up louder, and that's how we roll into the co-op parking lot — laughing and cranking the music at full volume. Like a normal, happy family.

Kind of like we used to be.

Confession:
I Think It Isn't Time to Give Up Yet

One night, when I was very small, I threw up in my bed. Then I threw up again. I called for my mom, but it was my dad who came in to check on me.

"I'm sick," I told him, and I started to cry.

"It's okay," Dad said. He came and hugged me, brushing my disgusting, vomity hair away from my face. Then he lifted me up and carried me to the bathroom. He gave me a bath, then went to clean my mattress and change my sheets. Dad washed my hair and combed it, then wrapped me in a towel. He changed me into some warm, fresh pajamas. Then he took me to the couch, where he wrapped me in a blanket and held me in his arms until I fell asleep again.

I still remember that. I remember how fresh and clean I felt. I was sick, but I was warm and safe.

That doesn't sound like someone who doesn't care about me, does it?

People make mistakes; they do the wrong thing. Sometimes they're annoying. Sometimes they're awful. (That's true for me, too, by the way.)

So how do you know when it's time to give up? And how do you know when to hang in there?

I guess you don't, really. You just make your choices and hope for the best.

Chocolate-Chip-Cookie Cupcakes
(makes approximately 12 cupcakes)

Did you know that cookies were invented by accident? They were originally just test bits of cake batter. So I'm just taking the cookie back to its roots.

INGREDIENTS:
- 1 cup milk
- 1 teaspoon apple cider vinegar
- 1/2 cup margarine or butter
- 1 cup dark brown sugar
- 2 tablespoons molasses
- 1 teaspoon vanilla extract
- 1-1/2 cups all-purpose flour
- 1 teaspoon baking powder
- 1/2 teaspoon baking soda
- 1/2 teaspoon salt
- 1/2 cup semisweet chocolate chips

INSTRUCTIONS:
1. Preheat the oven to 350°F. Line a muffin pan with cupcake liners.

2. In a small bowl, mix the milk and vinegar together and set aside to curdle for a few minutes.
3. In a large bowl, using a handheld mixer, cream the margarine or butter for a few minutes until lighter in color, then add the dark brown sugar and mix thoroughly. Add the curdled milk, molasses, and vanilla extract.
4. In another bowl, sift together the flour, baking powder, baking soda, and salt, and mix.
5. Add the dry ingredients to the wet ones a little bit at a time, and combine using a whisk or handheld mixer, stopping to scrape the sides of the bowl a few times, until no lumps remain. Add the chocolate chips and combine completely.
6. Fill cupcake liners two-thirds of the way and bake for 20–22 minutes. Transfer to a cooling rack, and let cool completely before frosting with your choice of frosting.

"So, what am I supposed to be thinking about when I look at this?" Marco asks as he studies the enormous metal sculpture. "Like, am I supposed to be having deep thoughts? Because all I'm thinking is that this is a giant Twinkie."

It *is* a giant Twinkie. It's bright yellow, and oozing some kind of metallic fake frosting. "Maybe you're supposed to be thinking about perspective," I say, but this is just a guess. I'm not really sure what this art is about, either. But I like it. "Wouldn't it be fun to get stuck inside that Twinkie, and have to eat your way out?"

Marco looks horrified. "That would be *awful*. I'd much rather get stuck inside a chocolate-chip cookie."

"Maybe a chocolate-chip-cookie cupcake?" I suggest.

"Definitely," he says, and we move on to the next sculpture. It's a giant Ring Ding. We stare at this awhile, until

Marco's phone chirps. He pulls it out, then types something quickly.

"Sorry," he mutters. "I'm meeting Tanisha later."

"Tanisha Osborne? Why?"

Marco shoves his phone back into his pocket. "She's going to tutor me in math."

"Oh," I say, and my heart lifts. Once Marco told Mr. Carter the truth about the cheating, I got my ninety-six back. With a warning, of course. And now my week of being grounded is over, and I'm hanging out with Marco.

"If I bring my grade up, I can probably rejoin the team in time for indoor soccer," Marco says.

"Are you missing it? The team, I mean?"

"Yeah. But I think I might start volunteering at Aurora Connection. Do you know about them?"

"They work with autistic kids?"

"Yeah." Marco moves away from the art and toward a series of sketches displayed on a wall near the window. The sketches are of crumbs . . . I think. "Anyway, maybe it's good that I'm getting a break from those guys." Marco's shoulder is turned toward me; I can't see his face. "Like Ezra." I remember how Marco and Ezra got into a huge fight a couple of months ago. I realize that Marco may have a point.

"Sometimes it's good to do something different. It gives you perspective."

"There's that word again," Marco says. "Did the Twinkies make you think of that?"

I remember Meghan's face framed against the blue sky as we looked down at the school yard. "No," I admit. "I was already thinking about it."

"Anyway, all those guys ever talk about is girls, movies, and sports." Marco turns to face me, and jerks his thumb toward the sculptures. "They never want to go look at Twinkie art."

"The funny thing about those Twinkies," I say as I stare at the sculpture, "is that they're actually kind of beautiful."

"Yeah . . ." He seems thoughtful. "Hayley —" He stops.

"What?"

Marco bites his lip, then gives his head a little shake. "I think I need a Twinkie."

"There's a shop down the street."

Marco grins. "Race you?"

Well, I'm sure you can guess what happens next. After all, I can never say no to Marco.

Acknowledgments

I would like to gratefully acknowledge the help of my sister, Zoë Papademetriou, who created the recipes in this book. I would also like to thank my editor Anamika Bhatnagar for her insight and input, my agent Rosemary Stimola for her unwavering enthusiasm, my husband for his willingness to listen to all of my thoughts and ideas, and my mother for her relentless support.

Bonus Recipe: Gluten-Free All-Purpose Flour

When a recipe calls for gluten-free all-purpose flour, I often recommend using Bob's Red Mill, but you can also easily make your own! Here are two variations to try.

INGREDIENTS FOR MIXTURE #1:
- 1/4 cup almond flour or coconut flour
- 1/3 cup white rice flour
- 1/3 cup quinoa flour or millet flour (millet is usually more affordable)
- 3 tablespoons tapioca flour
- 1 tablespoon ground flaxseeds

INGREDIENTS FOR MIXTURE #2:
- 2 cups sorghum flour
- 2 cups brown rice flour
- 1-1/2 cups potato starch (NOT potato flour)
- 1/2 cup white rice flour
- 1/2 cup sweet rice flour
- 1/2 cup tapioca flour
- 1/2 cup amaranth flour

1/2 cup quinoa or millet flour (millet is usually more affordable)

INSTRUCTIONS:
1. For either flour blend, sift each ingredient into a large mixing bowl. Thoroughly mix all ingredients together with a large whisk. Store the mix in a large covered container, either in the refrigerator or another cool, dark, and dry place. Label the container "Gluten-Free All-Purpose Flour Mix" to avoid confusion.
2. To use gluten-free (GF) all-purpose flour mixes, substitute your GF flour for all-purpose flour following a 1:1 ratio. (If the recipe calls for 1 cup of all-purpose flour, substitute 1 cup of GF flour.) You can add up to 1/4 cup more GF flour than directed if the batter consistency seems too watery.

Cannoli Cupcakes

(makes approximately 12 cupcakes)

INGREDIENTS:

- 1 cup soymilk
- 1 teaspoon apple cider vinegar
- 1-1/4 cups gluten-free all-purpose flour
- 3/4 teaspoon baking powder
- 1/2 teaspoon baking soda
- 1/2 teaspoon salt
- 1/3 cup granulated sugar
- 1/3 cup brown sugar
- 1/3 cup canola oil
- 1/2 teaspoon almond extract
- 1 teaspoon vanilla extract
- Pastry bag (or Ziploc bag)

INSTRUCTIONS:

1. Preheat the oven to 350°F. Line a muffin pan with cupcake liners.
2. In a medium bowl, whisk together the soymilk and vinegar, and set aside to curdle for a few minutes.

3. In another larger bowl, sift together the gluten-free flour, baking powder, baking soda, and salt.

4. Once the soymilk is curdled, add the granulated sugar and brown sugar, and mix thoroughly. Add the curdled soymilk, canola oil, and almond and vanilla extracts.

5. Add the dry ingredients to the wet ones a little bit at a time, and combine using a whisk or handheld mixer, stopping to scrape the sides of the bowl a few times, and mix until no lumps remain.

6. Fill cupcake liners two-thirds of the way and bake for 20–22 minutes. Transfer to a cooling rack, and let cool completely before frosting.

7. With your (clean!) thumb, poke large holes into the center of each cupcake. Alternately, take a small knife and carve out a cone from the center of each cupcake to create a well. (You can discard the cones, or eat them.)

8. Fill a pastry bag with Ricotta Frosting. (You can also make your own pastry bag by cutting off

a corner from a plastic Ziploc bag.) Insert the tip of the pastry bag into each cupcake, and squeeze it to fill the cavity you created. Then swirl the frosting on top of the cupcake to cover the opening.

Ricotta Frosting

INGREDIENTS:

2-1/2 cups whole-milk ricotta cheese

1-1/2 cups confectioners' sugar

1 teaspoon vanilla extract

3/4 cup miniature chocolate chips

Cheesecloth (or several layers of durable paper towels)

INSTRUCTIONS:

1. Take a bowl and place a wire mesh strainer inside it, then line the wire strainer with the cheesecloth (or paper towels). Add the ricotta cheese and place the bowl in the fridge, allowing it to strain for at least 2 hours, or overnight.

2. In a clean bowl, cream together the ricotta cheese and the confectioners' sugar, slowly adding the sugar in 1/2-cup batches, mixing completely before adding more.

3. Add the vanilla extract and miniature chocolate chips (as much or as little as you like, really), and beat on high speed until fluffy.